In the Shadow of their Dying

Michael R. Fletcher
& Anna Smith Spark

GdM

Acquiring Editor: Adrian Collins
Copy Editor: Sarah Chorn
Cover Artist: Carlos Diaz
Cover Design and Interior Layout: STK·Kreations

Hardcover ISBN: 978-0-6486635-2-2
Trade paperback ISBN: 978-0-6486635-3-9
eBook ISBN: 978-0-6486635-4-6
Worldwide Rights

First Edition, 2024

Published by Grimdark Magazine
Cammeray, NSW 2065
www.grimdarkmagazine.com

*To the Grimdark Fiction Readers and Writers
Facebook group for your continued support
and championing of the dark stuff.
This book in all its gritty glory is for you.*

CHAPTER ONE

THE THIRD BEST ASSASSIN

THE THIRD BEST assassin in Sharaam.

Who in the pale hells started negotiations with that? Who led with, "Since you're the third best assassin in the city…"

Someone about to low-ball your rate, Tash decided. *That's who.*

But Tash had been desperate and, let's face it, he was the third best assassin in a city no more than a week from being conquered by an invading army. The gates were closed, the walls manned. The harbour was crammed full of ships, but every time one tried to escape, the Tsarii blockade sank it. No one got in or out, unless you counted those soldiers falling from the wall.

A dozen flaming balls of pitch arced over the distant city wall to fall, sputtering, somewhere in the Taharishae District where all the politicians and Masters of Industry lived.

Couldn't happen to nicer people.

On good days the Tsarii threw rock and fire. On bad days it was alchemical sorcery, exploding clay orbs filled with nightmare narcotics, or bits of dead Sharaami soldiers.

Every night the Tsarii attacked, and every night the Sharaami soldiers sprinted to their stations to shove away scaling ladders or put out fires or get stabbed in the throat by someone scaling a ladder they'd been too slow to shove away. While there was plenty of killing going on in and around the city, there wasn't much demand for assassinations. For the most part, people who find themselves and all their most treasured enemies on the losing side of a siege don't bother hiring assassins to off their opponents. They're going to die anyway. Why waste money better spent drinking yourself senseless?

Moving door to door, shadow to shadow, Tash slid ever closer to the palace. A pair of guards passed in the street, chatting about whores they'd rut and whiskey they'd swill once their shift was over. They saw nothing.

Third best, my puckered arse.

The sky cracked, a jagged scar of blinding light forking across the heavens, illuminating an impenetrable dome of iron grey. The clouds loosed their water like a startled dog pissing and fat drops of icy rain hurtled toward the earth.

If it wasn't stone it was mud, and if it wasn't mud it was a pond. If not for the incessant rain, Sharaam might have been somewhere worth being.

Why do the Tsarii even want this miserable swamp?

On the other hand, if not for the incessant rain, the city would've burned to the ground in the first week of the war. No matter how much fire the Tsarii threw over the wall, it hissed and sizzled and died with a dejected sigh before managing to do much damage.

A roar of raised voices, a thunder a thousand times more terrifying than what followed the lightning, echoed in the streets as the Tsarii hurled themselves against the city. Apparently, they'd taken the lightning as a signal. It'd be funny, all that pointless death, if they weren't going to win. According to the soldiers he overheard drinking in The Dripping Bucket each night, the Tsarii army went on forever, blanketed the world all the way to the horizon.

Sharaam would fall, no doubt. The question was, how many would die before she did?

I'm saving lives, that's what I'm doing. History will remember me as noble. Selflessly heroic, even.

He'd sneak his third best arse into the palace, kill King Inshiil, and the war would be over. Not that Tash would be around to see it. Pitt, the man who hired him, had an escape route. A way out of the besieged city. Once Inshiil was dead, Tash would meet up with Pitt at The Dripping Bucket, collect his pay, and flee this doomed swamp.

South, he mused. Somewhere with sun, no invading armies, and women who find pasty pale skin exotic. That was real, right? Somewhere someone must find his dirty blond hair and sun-starved complexion attractive. Or just somewhere with sun, frankly. He couldn't imagine what it was like to be dry, for his toes not to be wrinkled prunes every moment of every day.

Come to think of it, why hadn't Qwneera or Geln taken the job? The pay might be substandard, like what you'd pay the third best rather than the first and second best, but the gig included guaranteed passage through the encircling army and away from Sharaam. Tash had heard both assassins were still here; neither escaped before the Tsarii invaded.

Weird thing about war: You don't believe it's going to happen until it's too rutting late.

Adjusting the pack he wore strapped tight to his back, Tash followed the guards. He moved like a ghost, flitting through shadows, perfectly silent. It was a total waste. They had to shout to hear each other over the downpour, and the wind out of the north whipped hard enough they were all but blind.

There were two more guards at the main entrance and the pair Tash followed stopped to chat. The four stood in the rain with their hoods pulled up, saving them from the worst of the onslaught but also killing their peripheral vision. Slipping past them, he tiptoed through the clinging muck of a flower garden where only nettles and weeds grew. Every footstep squelched like a sucking chest wound. Reaching the wall, he scraped the worst of the mud off his shoes and climbed to the first balcony. Picking the lock, he let himself in, closing the door behind him.

The room was, as Pitt claimed it would be, an abandoned library. White sheets draped empty bookshelves and luxurious chairs and sofas. This was a good start. If the weaselly little bastard got all the details correct, maybe Tash wouldn't die here.

Tash shed his black rain-slick and stood listening. Thunder, muted by the closed door, rumbled loud enough to rattle windows.

He slid the pack off and withdrew the servant's uniform, laying it neatly on the floor. Next, he stripped out of his damp clothes—no rain slick in the world was enough to keep the weather of Sharaam out—and donned the dry servant's clothing. Not a bad fit. A little snug across the shoulders, but not so much anyone would comment. He checked that the blade strapped to the small of his back didn't show an unsightly bulge giving itself away.

Acceptable.

Too easy. Just the way he liked it.

Did Qwneera and Geln know something he didn't? Or maybe they'd made other arrangements to escape the city before the walls fell. Certainly, both were wealthy enough. But the prestige! Killing the king would put Tash in their ranks, maybe even displace one of them. He imagined Pitt calling Qwneera the "third best assassin" to her face. The rat-bastard would die a fraction of a second later, but the look on her face—the knowledge she'd been surpassed—would more than make it worthwhile.

Closing his eyes, he imagined the palace floorplan. The king's chambers were two floors up in the eastern wing. Tash would stop by the kitchen on this floor, collect a tray of food, and then play at delivering it to the king. Knife in the brain, collect the signet from King Inshiil's right hand as proof, and then back here to slip out the same way he crept in. Meet Pitt at The Dripping Bucket, a dozen blocks away, and collect his money. By tomorrow morning Tash would be safely outside the walls and on his way south. Really, it didn't take a genius to work out who Pitt was working for.

Kill the king.

Passage out of a city surrounded by a massive army.

Tash didn't love the idea of working for the Tsarii but he liked the idea of dying even less. And gold was gold and King Inshiil could go rut himself with that silly iron sceptre he always carried. If he'd been a better king, they wouldn't be in this damned mess in the first place.

Time to kill.

Tash crossed to the door and opened it, ready to stride casually from the library like he'd been in there for a perfectly good reason.

A young woman stood in the hallway facing him, like she'd been waiting to come in, too polite to knock and interrupt whatever he'd been about. At barely five feet, she was a full foot shorter than Tash and plump like the women who worked the bakery he visited each morning. She blinked up at him, a lazy eye not quite managing to achieve focus. She wore a loose brown smock, which, considering the colour of her hair, eyes, and her already potato-like shape, was a terrible choice.

"Umm," Tash said, stepping to one side as if to either let her into the room or slip past her. "Pardon me?"

She glanced past him, taking in the abandoned library. His gut soured. If she questioned him, he'd have to kill her. He slid a hand back to touch the hilt of the knife strapped to the small of his back. She turned her attention to him. Or maybe she did. He couldn't tell which eye was doing the seeing.

"If I may?" he said, making as if to pass.

She didn't move.

Was she staring at his throat?

She's simple, been hit in the head or something.

A faint hint of rot teased his nose. Was that coming from the kitchen?

"If I could just…" He nodded at the hall behind her.

She didn't move, showed no sign of having heard or understood.

"I have chores," he tried. "Tasks to complete."

She sniffed at him, petite nose upturned. Leaning in, she drew a deep whiff of his armpit like a dog sniffing someone's crotch.

"Umm…" Definitely not right in the head. "If you could… just… maybe… step aside?"

Killing a king was one thing. It was a thing he was being paid to do, and it was a thing that would get him the hell out before the Tsarii put everyone's head on a spike for not believing the right thing about something he wasn't clear on. Or maybe it was about trade routes. But: you didn't get to be the best assassin of even a cold, wet cow turd like Sharaam by killing everyone who crossed your path. But again: the longer he let her keep him trapped in this abandoned library, the more likely someone less dim-witted would come along and wonder what in the palest hell was going on.

What is that smell?

Frustrated, Tash stepped back. "Come on in." Holding the door open, he waved her into the room.

Once in, he'd close the door, crack her on the back of the head—hopefully not further addling her brain—and go about his business.

The woman stepped into the library, leaning to glance past him at his pack and the sodden change of clothes crumpled on the floor. Had she been smarter and not so obviously soft in the head, he'd worry about her figuring things out. As it was, she showed no hint of concern or understanding.

Even the third best assassin can get past a simple serving wench without resorting to murder.

"Third best," she said as if he'd spoken aloud.

"I'm sorry?"

"Not third best."

She was speaking nonsense.

"Do you like books?" Tash asked, gesturing toward a bookcase, hoping she'd glance that way and he could whack her on the head or maybe choke her to unconsciousness.

That lazy eye did a greasy slide to focus on the bookshelf while the other continued to stare at his chest. Her breath carried a carrion waft, the subtlest hint of decaying meat.

Bleah. Chew a mint leaf or something.

She grinned flat little teeth.

"Not third best," she repeated, "if Qwneera and Geln are dead."

She focused both eyes on his face and suddenly he wished she hadn't. Fear thrummed through him, turned his bowels to water. The overpowering stench of decay filled the abandoned library.

Tash drew his knife and stabbed her in the throat with one perfectly smooth, much-practised, movement. Or at least that's what he meant to do. She swayed away, bending backward in a way that made him want to retch. He stabbed again, feinting high and going low to drive the blade into her heart. Again she twisted, sinuous like she had a snake's spine. She took his knife, plucked it from his fingers, and tossed it aside.

"Oh," said Tash.

Then he ran, sprinted for the door he'd entered the palace through. Shouldering it aside, he skidded on the rain-slicked stone of the balcony, hit the railing, and flipped over it with a scream. He landed badly on one shoulder, the mud of the flower garden saving him from shattered bones but still crushing the breath from him.

Rolling to his feet, Tash sprinted, wheezing, for the street. Raised voices and yelling guards followed him. Daring a glance over his shoulder he saw the lumpy little woman standing, backlit, in the library. She watched him, head tilted to one side. While the guards searched about in the dark, chasing shadows, he knew she saw him.

Tash ran. Every footstep squelched loud, calling out his progress. He tasted grit and mud and his skull ached. His head must have impacted alongside his shoulder. He hadn't noticed. Nasty things hissed past him in the dark, the evil sound of crossbow bolts cutting through a heavy rain. He ducked and dodged, hurled himself around the first corner, and ran faster.

Pitt was a fucking dead man. He'd already hired Qwneera and Geln to kill the king and they both failed. Then, when he hired Tash—who was now, by definition, the best assassin in Sharaam—he spewed that shit about him being third to cut his rate.

I'm going to gut him.

Or he would if he still had a knife.

I'll choke him until his eyeballs pop.

Flaming balls of pitch, sputtering sparks like shooting stars, arced over the outer wall and fell tumbling into the city. If you were unlucky enough to be hit by one, you were dead. Otherwise, they were more a nuisance than anything. Right now, they lit the streets Tash fled down and that was definitely annoying. Dozens of guttering fires fought to raze Sharaam and lost their war with the rain.

Tash ran.

Dark alleys and abandoned buildings.

He ran until his lungs gave out and then he cowered in the burnt-out wreck of a hospital until he got his breath back. No one found him. No mousey pudge with a greasy sliding eye wandered into the wreckage to expose him.

I didn't imagine that. I'm not overreacting.

How in the pale hells could he explain this to Pitt without the bastard making fun of him for fleeing from a servant?

He remembered the way she leaned forward to sniff at his armpit, a dog catching the scent of its prey.

"Oh, fuck fuck fuck."

She wasn't some addled serving wench. Her spine, the way she moved and bent. Those eyes watching him, watching everything. "Not third," she had said, just after he thought about being third. Had he imagined that? Had it been coincidence?

She killed Qwneera and Geln, he knew it in his blood. She killed the two best assassins in Sharaam, and Pitt sent him in without a word of warning or even mentioning, "Oh hey, two assassins—both better than you—died trying to collect this mark."

Fucker!

Breathing under control, he forced himself into motion. Tempting as spending the rest of the night hiding in the wreckage was, there was a time limit here. The deal was that he killed the king, and Pitt got him out tonight. For reasons Tash neither knew nor gave a flying sewer-rat's scrotum for, the window of opportunity on leaving Sharaam closed at dawn.

He'd find Pitt and Pitt would get him the hell out of the city or he'd kill the bastard. Speaking of killing, he'd have to find a new knife. Maybe Pitt could get him one. He had a way of finding things that bordered on magical.

If he gets me a knife and gets me out, I'll only kill him a little.

No way Tash was going to collect the bounty—what with the king being so inconveniently not dead—but he had to get out. He didn't want to be in the city when the walls fell and the Tsarii came pouring in. But even more so, he didn't want to be trapped in Sharaam as long as that woman was in here with him.

Woman? Right. What in the pale hells was she?

Tash headed for The Dripping Bucket, sticking to the back alleys and avoiding the regularly patrolled streets. Having to pick his way through shattered buildings blocking his route slowed his progress. Tsepsis Street was a wreck. Last week a stone the size of a large bear had somehow been launched over the wall and tumbled through several buildings. It crushed a theatre and an orphanage and ploughed a knee-deep trench across the road which immediately filled with muddy water. The stone had come to rest in a church after smashing through the altar, which seemed fitting. Word was the pastor lay crushed beneath it.

Good to know the gods aren't picking favourites.

Tash jumped and twitched at every sound, expecting that little woman to step out of the dark at any moment and explain why he was no longer the third best assassin. By the time he reached The Dripping Bucket he was sodden and shivering, still wearing his palace servant's uniform. What a terrible night! He'd lost his knife, his best rain slick, his pack, and his work clothes with all the concealed pockets. If only the little bitch'd showed up earlier, before he'd changed. How long had she been waiting at the door for him? How had she known?

Pitt sent me in exactly the same way he sent the other two!

That had to be it.

I'm going to swap his balls for his eyes and he can spend the rest of his life staring at his own hairy arse.

Pushing through the front door, Tash stood dripping, surveying the inn's patrons. All the usual detritus were present and correct. Mar, a young man with insane and very tedious delusions he was once someone important. And Flet. Both perfectly nice, perfectly normal people, far too nice and normal for the cesspit that was the Bucket, except for the endless horrible stories they both dribbled out when over-excited. Acol, a knackered ex-soldier who never stopped banging on about how he'd manage the war effort. Sharaam would have defeated Tsarr in two days with no casualties if the higher-ups had only deigned to listen to Acol's specialist professional management advice: "what they need to do, right, our side, what we need to do is kill the Tsarii before they kill us."

Casey, a local thief who now stole solely to support his headlong descent into alcoholic dementia, twitched as Tash entered. Seeing it was Tash, he went back to scraping at the tabletop with the tip of his dagger. Casey wore that haunted look he always had when not yet drunk enough. In the space of a few weeks the man had gone from being a successful thief to attempting death by drink. He always sat alone, always scratched at the tabletop with his dagger, always flinched in fear when the door to The Dripping Bucket swung open. He never said why, never talked about what had happened.

A few patrons glanced up, noted Tash's entrance, acknowledged or ignored him depending on their history, and returned to their business.

Tash nodded at Casey as he passed but the thief had returned to his work on the tabletop. Glancing down, Tash saw the carving of a heavyset woman cut into the wood. Casey, it turned out, was a talented artist.

Tash stopped. He knew that shape, that potato in a brown frock, that crudely cut mousey hair. Casey had even captured the way one eye wandered.

"You know her?" Tash asked.

"Bound," said Casey, not looking up from his work. "The king's sceptre."

"What? The woman, do you know the woman?"

"Tried to steal it."

"Who is she?"

"All the pale hells," slurred Casey.

Cursing, Tash left the man to his drink and his carving. Clearly drunk, the thief made no sense.

Three rusty oil lanterns hung from twists of steel, lighting the room a jaundiced yellowy brown.

Katch worked the bar, pouring watered whiskey, horse-piss beer, and the vinegar he laughingly referred to as wine. His wife, Jaan, worked the floor, waddling her fat arse between tables and badgering people to buy more drinks or get the fuck out.

Of Pitt there was nothing to be seen. His usual table was empty.

It's okay. I'm early. He wouldn't expect me to be back so soon.

Tash stalked across the room, nodding at those he recognized as worth acknowledging and ignoring the rest. He sat at Pitt's table, taking the bastard's seat so he could keep his back to the wall and his eyes on the entrance. It also placed him close to the door at the back that folks used when ducking out to piss in the alley.

Always know your exits.

Jaan sidled up to the table, face flushed and florid, beady eyes examining him from under a sweaty mop of curly blond hair.

"Whatcha drinking, Tash?"

Rutting hells, he'd left his coin purse in his pack back at the palace. *Pitt will spot me a round.*

"Whiskey. Double."

"You eating?"

If he didn't order food, she'd kick him off the table to leave it open for more profitable patrons. He didn't want to stand at the bar or the long shelf lining the wall. He'd done enough running today.

"Yeah. What's dinner?"

"Pie."

What Jaan called pie was closer to a sludgy stew with a piece of dark bread thrown atop. The fact she didn't mention the kind of meat meant it was one of those days where you were better off not knowing. Dog. Rat. Cat. Sewer snake. Or something worse.

"Fine. Pie. And a pint of ale." As long as Pitt was paying, Tash might as well have himself a meal.

He watched Jaan waddle away, her colossal arse bumping tables. The only person he'd ever met with a bigger arse was Katch and he kept his hidden behind the bar.

Simonsi, a failed alchemist who sold shoddy cures and immunizations to all the strange shit the Tsarii threw over the wall, sat in her usual place near Pitt's table. Midnight hair and obsidian eyes, she possessed the most fantastically shaped lips. She and Tash had been together for a while, but she left him for reasons he never understood. No one in all his life kissed like Simonsi.

Seeing Tash, she said, "You hear about the Mother of Ashton Nunnery?"

His heart skipped. She usually ignored him. "No. What happened?"

She leaned across the space between them and he smelled the alchemical residue of whatever concoction she last worked on commingled with the rose-scented shampoo she used.

"Tsarii munitions. Clay pots loaded with a blend of hallucinogens, disinhibitors, and muscle enhancers. The nuns went crazy, started screaming about demons and attacking everyone. The Watch had to put them down. Over three hundred dead between the nuns and the guard." She examined him, beautiful lips pursed. "I have an immunization that will protect—"

Ah. That's why you're talking to me. "I'm broke." Not to mention he was hoping to escape this hell tonight. *If we were still together, I'd bring you with me.* But she'd already turned away, returning to a conversation with the woman she shared a table with.

Tash cursed under his breath. Why did she get to move on so easily? Why did he have to sit here thinking about her lips and wondering what in all the pale hells he did wrong?

If I told her I was leaving Sharaam tonight, would she come with me? Doubtful.

Someone at the bar started singing in a whiskey-rasped voice. Something about obsidian hearts, made brittle with time, shattering at the loss of a love. In moments half the room took up the song and Tash decided they were all lucky he didn't still have a knife.

The whiskey came first, and he banged that back with a grimace. Even watered down it tasted like the armpit of a dead Septuu clansman who'd been left to rot in a peat bog for at least a week. The pie came next, steaming hot, with that slab of dark bread thrown atop like just by having something bready nearby magically transformed it from stew to pie. Tash didn't care. He ate fast, shovelling food into his mouth the instant the previous mouthful had been mostly swallowed.

He thought while he ate. Pitt would be here soon. How would the pug-ugly weasel-rapist react to news of Tash's failure?

Well, he won't be happy.

And he wasn't going to want to pay up either, in spite of the fact that he pretty much sent Tash to certain death. Would Pitt still be willing to smuggle him out of the city?

Pretty fucking unlikely.

As far as Tash saw, he had one thing on his side: He knew Pitt hired three assassins to kill King Inshiil. Either Pitt got him out of

Sharaam, or Tash was going to drop a few key words in the right ears and Pitt was going to enjoy getting a look at the surrounding army from atop a spike.

The floor shook as a trebuchet-tossed rock landed somewhere nearby, likely tumbling through a few lives and leaving wreckage in its wake. For a score of heartbeats the room stilled, drinks raised partway to open mouths as everyone waited. Sometimes the Tsarii liked to drop a bunch of rocks on the same neighbourhood. Someone out on the street screamed, a broken wail of agony. When nothing fell from the sky to end their lives, the patrons of The Dripping Bucket returned to the task of drinking themselves to death.

Tash sipped his pint.

What if he told Pitt he'd succeeded, but that the guards arrived before he had a chance to grab the signet? Would he believe him? Would it be enough to get him out of the city? Maybe he could magnanimously waive his fee—seeing as he couldn't offer proof of death—as long as they left immediately.

The door swung open, and Tash glanced up, hoping it was Pitt. Three soldiers staggered in, two men and a woman. Having served his time in the army, like every Sharaami youth, he knew the type. They'd stayed in for the uniform and the pay, confident no one was dumb enough to want to conquer Sharaam. Unlike these three, Tash got out the instant he served his minimum time.

The soldiers weaved drunkenly between tables on their way to the bar, bumping into more than they avoided. They'd likely been ejected from their previous booze hole. Mud caked their uniforms. Even drunk as lords, barely able to order a round of drinks, Tash saw the broken look in their eyes. They'd seen death. A lot of death. They'd seen friends stabbed or pulled from the wall to fall to the rocks below. They'd seen agony and horror as they pushed their swords into the meat of enemy soldiers. Heard the screams of the wounded, watched the surgeons saw off limbs. Seen the shallow trench-graves filled with the fallen, the crushed, the burnt. They knew that tomorrow it might be them falling from the wall or feeling a Tsarii spear slide into their guts. They knew tomorrow might see their corpses tossed carelessly into a trench grave.

The stench of spilled entrails and the rot of death followed them everywhere, filled their every moment, haunted their dreams.

The thought reminded Tash of the woman, the faint odour of decay haunting her. The greasy slide of that eye.

"Not the third," like she heard his thoughts.

Damn it, Pitt! Where in the pale hells are you?

He had to get out. He had to get out now.

One of the oil lanterns lighting the room guttered and went out. The other two flickered and sputtered.

Tash imagined he caught the faintest hint of decaying meat in the air.

The front door swung open.

Please be Pitt. Please be Pitt.

The greasy-eyed woman walked in. Alone. Short, and unassuming, tented in that frumpy frock. No one even noticed her. So normal. Mousey brown hair, bangs cut straight above brown eyes. And then one of those eyes slid away to examine the bar while the other surveyed the room.

Casey twitched and stood. "I didn't take it," he said, pleading, eyes wide and terrified. "I didn't know."

Tash's heart stopped. His chest tightened.

Get up. Run away.

Except he didn't want to move, didn't want to draw attention to himself.

One eye found Casey.

The other slid, greasy and slick, until it focussed on Tash.

Casey shook with terror. "Not like the others," he begged. "Please."

He seemed to discover some deep well of bravery and straightened, eyes hard. If he was drunk, Tash saw none of it in him. The thief moved toward the woman, knife appearing in his hand as if by magic. He was the fastest blade Tash ever saw. And then Casey lay sprawled on the floor, body rigid and shaking, vibrating impossibly fast. If she touched him, Tash missed it.

Casey stilled, blood spilling from every orifice, leaking from his eyes and ears. The growing pool moved, wriggled like worms, seethed like snakes.

The Dripping Bucket fell silent.

Pushing back from the table, Tash stood.

The second eye slid until both focussed on him.

The other two lanterns flickered and guttered, plunging the tavern into darkness.

The sweet hint of putrescence.

Tash ran.

CHAPTER TWO

IANANR THE BOUND ONE

FIND IT.

Kill it.

It ran. It ran from me. Filth thing, with its filth purge perfume scent, white face thing like a fish belly, maggot eyes thing vile thing, it ran away. Nothing gets away.

I am a hunter. I am bound to my duty. With smoke and chains and words my master bound me, I lay in sleep, warm in warm soft blood-fire dozing dreaming, the old times when we were all that lived to walk the earth, I dreamed of that time, the yearning for it growing, hot pulse in my crotch. My master gathered smoke and chains in the darkness, spoke words of power, summoned me, chained me, bound me, and I am bound to hunt and kill. Weak disease thing my master. Bound me. Trapped me.

It ran. It cannot escape me.

I slide down into the darkness of the streets of Sharaam, unpronounceable name in their ugly babbling tongue. It means 'City of the Great', my master told me proudly, as though that might mean something to me. Pitiful buildings of crude stone crouched on rot-mud. They shit into the filth, they bury their dead in the filth, they need the rot-mud to live. They raise their buildings, think them beautiful, and now they die here fighting over them. They are pathetic things. They deserve butchery and slaughter, in the times long past they ran to our call, we controlled them. If I was free of these word-chains, I would kill them.

My master bound me with word-chains to its weak vile will. I am a hunter. Kill.

"They will try to harm the king. You will not allow them to harm the king. You will stop them." Words like wounds opening. Itching burning scoring across this body until it is done.

"If the king dies, Iananr…"

Bound. Kill it. Now. Hunt. Go.

* * *

IANANR MOVED THROUGH the city of Sharaam. Wandering. Walking. Frail on heavy legs. The awkwardness of this body. Unpleasant to move. Unpleasant to see. Not been out in the city before, beyond the walls of the castle they bound her in. Staring and strange. Looking for the colour trail her prey had left behind it, running. The narrow city streets in the rain-shadow, the stones of the buildings glistening with rain, the buildings and the sky and the city walls all blurring. The red light of fires, the city burning, making the world darker, making her vision flicker. Patterns like blood clots where alchemical workings poured and splashed. Over that, the other world that was easier to see, but in which the city itself could not be seen. She had to hold her eyes open to see all of it. There: traces, ebbing colours, ink-in-water, the prey, running. Down a narrow street, all rubble and garbage. Round a corner, scramble over a broken-down wall, down a wide street with the wind blowing rain full in her face. A troop of soldiers went past her, heading for the walls. Rain dripping down their armour. Death clawing beating at them. A roar from off to the east, a missile hitting the walls or the gates. In her other eyes she saw it flash like spark light. Green and silver. Taste of magic. She saw the stone of the walls shriek.

"The more of our lot the Tsarii kill now, the more glory there'll be for us that's left when we take them down," the soldier that would die first said to its comrades. "Doing us that survive to kill them a fucking favour, yeah? Rewards and promotions all round."

"Yeah!" shouted the one that was longing to die.

They walked faster when they saw Iananr. Sensed something. She turned her head to watch them splashing away through the rain.

Voices. Strain to hear them. Understand them.

"When this is over... when this is over, I'm going to sleep for a bloody week."

"When this is over... when this is over, I'm going to stay indoors by a fire for a fucking month."

"Remember last summer, when we were all worried about a sodding drought?"

Iananr thought: They are... afraid. Of dying.

Strange.

Tumbled buildings, houses with barred windows, everywhere the smell of smoke. A white face stared down at her from a hole like the hole in a skull, disappeared back. Another face, beside it, staring up at the sky. There were leaves around the window they looked from. Plants growing there. And a shopfront below, boarded up, full of shining gold all scattered. A faint ghost hint of a man's blood. There had been joy here. The women up above had been weeping. Things had been done.

Iananr smiled a pleasure smile a hunger smile. Enjoy it. Feel. Things hungered here. This place was how our whole world was.

Word-chains. Find it. Hunt it. Follow the trail. Go on. She walked through streets where the people of the city had been dying. Through streets where they crouched alive in fear. Soldiers in the walls, staring out, coughing, searching, "When will they come? Oh gods, oh gods, when?" Barricades in the streets, broken by the army outside's bombardment. Pools of petty magic, alchemical sweetness, stop and taste it, drink. Everything shattered up.

Green fire and blue fire and great lumps of stonework. Killing things and hurting things. The army outside the walls hurled them at the city and the city howled on and on. She almost understood it. The fear in the people of the city, in the army outside, the shame, the horror, the desire. Iananr thought: They enjoy it.

A man came up to her. Not a soldier. Came close to her. Looked at her with bared teeth. There was violence in it. Wet hunger. It wanted. Like the hands that had pawed over the scattered bloodied gold in the boarded-up ransacked shop.

Strain to hear it. Understand it. "Hey, girl," it said. "What you got?"

It moved itself at her and she reached out at it. Unloosed herself. Clawed at it. It was so weak.

Iananr thought: It wants to hurt this body. Why should it want that?

She felt the last of it at her feet dying. It had hurt as it died, and that as always surprised her. Why should it feel? She squatted next to its body, reached out plump fingers, touched it. The eyes staring up towards her. The mouth open. Red skin visible inside the mouth. She placed her face very close to it. Breathed it in. Warm inside her. Sweet and fresh and good. Lapped the blood carefully. Sweet. Opened her mouth, her real mouth, opened up rows and rows and rows of teeth. She sighed with almost-pleasure when she had finished. A little dry patch of colour, vivid, on the bare ground. She breathed out with a hiss and the colour was gone. All gone. Nothing left of the dead thing. Never been.

Iananr went on.

The prey's trail went off to the west, away from the walls. Sadly, she turned to follow it. Down a smaller street, lined with houses piled in together; she could feel people and rats and lice, see the walls of the buildings itching with life. The street opened into a courtyard, a well at the centre. Iananr snorted in disgust at the feel of the water. Pain worse than the itch of the word-chains. Cold pain. Felt her mouth writhe, could almost taste the water. The prey's trail went up to the well, hung around the well bucket. Iananr edged around the walls of the courtyard, keeping away. There was a tree growing in the courtyard and that also confused her, confused her vision. Not good to try to look at, even now with the life running out of it. It was very bright, like a tower of fire, it confused her, cast shadows in the city world and the real world. She went past it quickly, holding her breath to stop herself having to breathe the feel of it. It would be good if the war machines could hit it, splinter and burn it.

On the other side of the courtyard a building was burning, was broken open, it must have been hit by one of the missiles thrown by the army outside the walls. There was a child's body on the ground in front of it. A girl child, the thing like a face all burned. Broke up the colour lines of her true seeing. Her prey had stepped over the child and had felt pain then. The child had perhaps come from the house.

Her prey had gone down a narrow alley. She could not see the sky at all here, the buildings bent over towards each other, falling into each other. Her feet slipped on the wet ground. Everything here was rot and filth. People had died in this alley, many of them, once. There were bones there beneath the ground. Coming loose as the rain fell and the earth turned to black mud; they would float upwards in the mire, be revealed. Dry bones that yearned to feel rain and sun and air.

The city would fall before that. Other deaths would choke the alley. The buildings would fall over all of it.

Something stopped her moving. A crawling shrieking burning pain in her arm. Revulsion. Her mind and her vision white with disgust. A man, burned like the child, a wound on it, clutching at her arm.

"Help me." Slurred speech. "Please."

She shouted, "Get away from me." Hard to speak in this word-language. Too crude and too complex. The man was pulling at her arm, shouting, blood pouring out of it. Stopping her from following her prey. It stank of dying: stop and watch it stop and watch it, this whole filth city, everywhere she went there was dying, it drummed in her. Be loose here, wander, stand on the walls, watch and feel the dying. Taste it, sense it. Pleasure heat building up in her, spread herself out over the city feel it take it taste it wallow in it. Hot pain of the man's hand gripping her. Disgusting.

"Help me. Please." The other hand flapping towards the well. "Water. Please."

Word-chains closing on her. The prey. Kill it. Find it. The prey's scent trail fading now. Caught up in the dying around her, the burning house, the well and the tree that sickened her. Too many smells and senses. Getting blurred. I'm tired, master. I was sleeping. Eternities passed and I slept. This place is no longer a world for me. Too much. Too different. I crouch as a guardian, I am a watcher in the night; implacable I watch over my charge, protecting it, shielding it. I am like a shield I am like armour, I do not need to rest. I sit beside it to protect. If the word-chains break I will… Oh, my master, oh my charge, I watch for a flaw in the word-chain, if the word-chain breaks

I will glut myself on you, I will have such pleasures with you. Feel it. Clutch it. Rub at it. Wet in my body, spreading. This false body. My real body. Sweet pain filth. But it's not real. Pretending. Wet pleasuring fades to shame. Protect. Guard it. I am bound I cannot kill them. Find the prey. Kill the prey.

"Help me."

Iananr shook its flesh hand off her body. "Get away." She said in the word-language voice, "Where is it? Where is it?"

It drew back from her. Seemed to see her. It was oozing with fear now. White fear running down its face and hands. "Oh gods… gods… mercy." The last word a scream.

It sees me.

The scream was beautiful music. The idiot thing her prey had not understood her, wrapped up in its dreams, blind to everywhere that was not itself. This man saw and understood. She had trampled a world filled with screams once, when all was younger. Human voices pleading, and she had danced over them, filled herself with them, soaked them into her skin. Garbed herself in human screams.

The word-chains bit into her. The trail. Follow the prey's trail. She twisted back and forth, searching. Smell and sight and feel. The smell of it, the traces of it, colour-taste in the air. This world and the real world. These eyes and her real eyes. Where is it gone? It cannot escape me. Flickerings in the air, faint scent-memories: it was here, the last time the sun was risen, or the night before that, or the night before that again. She could see the shadow of it, where it had walked in the past, where it might walk in the future. The trail it left now was lost.

My master will be angry. Will punish me.

Filth shame ruin rage wet pleasure, that she was reduced to fear of punishment.

"Your duty is to protect King Inshiil, Iananr. Your one duty. Whatever comes, a lone man or the whole Tsarii army, you will protect him.

I bind you to him. Do you understand? If you understand, Iananr, nod your head."

Humiliation. Rage. I scream and roar, thrash against the word-chains, spill myself in fire at it. It stands over me and it is afraid, I know it is afraid, it is shocked by my power, how close I am to shattering the bindings it has wrapped around me. I scream curses, I tell it what I shall do to it. What it will suffer, when the word-chains break.

"Your duty, Iananr. I command you." Its voice is shaking. "I command you, Iananr."

The word-chains lash at me. Burn me. They are too strong.

"My duty," I whisper. "Master."

It croons with pleasure. It is enjoying its fear of me, my rage-fear of it.

* * *

IT MUST BE here! The trail! The prey cannot escape! Iananr got down on her knees, awkward in this awkward flesh-rot disease body, sniffing the ground, staring, searching. The rainwater cold and vile, burning her real skin. Pain-flesh. Blind and haltered. No trace.

She went back to the dying man. Took it apart to sate herself. Calm a little of her anger. Bury her shame at failing. Layers and layers of blood and pain and dying. Sinking down into them. Such a weak thing, and dying; she stood in the filthy alley, on the bones of others long-dead, did not feel calmed or less ashamed.

The feel of the air was changing. The rain slacking. She felt less solid in the light. More confused. The city world was more real, her own world fainter. Harder to see and think. Go back to the palace, she thought. Guard the king. But her master would be angry.

"It's lost, it's gone, it won't come back," she said aloud in her own language in her own mouth. The tree in the courtyard snapped and shuddered at her voice, the branches rattled like bones, dead leaves falling, the water in the well hissed in steam.

She said aloud, "I have killed two of them already. This one is a coward, it will not come back to trouble the king again." The child's dead body and the man's dead body jerked at her voice. Decay spreading over them, their faces crumbling away green and black. Perfume: half-unaware of what she was doing, she breathed deep, filled herself with the scent. Grave worms hatching and dying in the dead flesh. It called itself "the third best assassin". She had heard it call itself that, loud in its head; it was proud-ashamed of the name. Both the pride and the shame she had tasted, smelled on it. It knew she had killed the others, "first best" and "second best", "Qwneera" and "Geln" they had called themselves in their hearts as she killed them. It was afraid because she had killed better things than it. It was afraid of her.

The child's body and the man's body decaying at her voice. Writhing puddles of filth and grave worms. The worms sang of the pleasure of corpse-flesh. Their colour trails fading, every trace of them in this world eaten away by her voice.

The word-chains bit into her. Tight pain. Tried to enjoy it. Tried and tried, since her master had bound her. Hurt too deep, too much. Trapped.

Kill it.

* * *

A LONG WALK, trailing through the streets. The rain became lighter. Felt like the breath of the woman Qwneera gasping out on her face warm and soft and hateful, as Iananr killed and consumed it. Made her skin itch. The things camped beyond the walls slacked off their killing games a brief while. People out on the streets, white-faced, wide-eyed, creeping out from their attempts at shelter now the bombardment was briefly at an end. Examining the damage done. Mourning the dead. They still tried to live, some of them, tried to buy and sell, visit their friends, prepare food to celebrate things. As if the city would survive. It delighted her. The sense of their hope. The beating dark beyond it of their knowledge they were lying to themselves. The certainty, beyond the despair, that they could not die even if every other man, woman and child in the city died, because...

A child stopped to stare at her from a doorway. She was going too fast. Moving out of step with the body that she wore. The child saw something wrong in her. She stared back at the child and smiled at it. Its eyes opened wide. Iananr beckoned it over. Another little girl, very thin.

"Where are your parents?" Iananr asked it carefully. Get the words right. Speak in the right tongue.

"Dead," the child said. "A clay pot came down, really small thing, hit the house and they're dead. Spare a coin? It won't matter if you give me a coin, will it? In a few days when you're dead and I'm dead." It knew that. Young as it was. But it believed, also, young as it was, that if it said the city would fall, that it would die—it believed like so many of them that saying that truth could make it untrue.

A coin appeared in Iananr's hand. Gold. She dropped the coin into the child's palm and its eyes widened.

Iananr touched the child's face. The child's eyes closed. Opened again.

Red gleam in its eyes. It smiled at Iananr. Licked its dirty, thin lips. Walked away down the street.

I should not have done that.

But...

Pleasing.

And the bombardment of the city was starting again. The army outside grinding them down. For... something. Bright light, green and blue fire. A shriek, a scream, from far off beyond the walls she felt a shout and a cheer of triumph. Iananr walked carefully on.

* * *

IN AN ALLEYWAY, Iananr stopped walking. Voices and shouting, food smells, sweat. A gathering place. A woman asleep in the gutter, grey hair in a pool of piss.

Here!

Faint. Rippling. Scent-trails, colour-trails, tracing out. Unspooling. Faint as whispers. Almost lost in all the rest. Here! It was. It will be. It knows this place.

Two men talking, around the corner. Strain to hear them. Piss stink of them. The ghost of the scent trail on them. Hope! Pitiful, in one such as her kind. We did not have to hope once, we did not have to search, we were everything. They were talking, plotting, pissing out into the dirt. "We'll meet back here." And they had the scent, the colours, faint on them. Kill them. Make them tell. In her shame she wavered. Make them tell! They can't know, they won't know, the prey has escaped her. She's failed. Wading through the world unmatched and now she has failed in it. She spat and tore and pleasured herself, running liquid shame in the blind weight of her false masker's body. It crushed at her, shamed her, how little and nothing it felt. The men went off, the ghost of the scent trail, her delusion that they knew her failure.

They knew. They knew.

Ran. Fled after it. One of them. It knew. Traces in it, scent-trails. It knew. She came up on it and it wheeled round at her, big thing like a wall, all pounded meat.

"What? What do you want?" Ugly sneer look on its face.

It had killed things. Iananr thought: Blood and death. Killing. Oh, it enjoys it.

Iananr thought: Axe.

It said, "What?" in its ugly tongue.

Say it in this word-language. Hard. Too complex, too simple. She said, "I am... looking... for a... a man."

"Aren't we bloody all, woman? Now get out."

She said, "Tell me." Looked at it. There, in its mind. It knew the prey. The prey's colour trail, coiling, touch it, smell it, taste it.

The man swayed. "Tash," it said. Slow fearful voice. Didn't say. Thought it. These creatures' thoughts were so loud like speaking in their crude ugly word-language. "Tash."

She saw the thing's face in its mind. The third-best assassin. The prey.

Tash.

"Where? I'm looking for it. Lost it. Where is it?"

"I don't... don't know."

"Where is it?"

Colour traces in its head. Its bowels opened. It came down its leg with a gasp and a grunt and a stink. "I don't know. I don't know. I don't know."

Kill it. She stripped her claws to gut it, flay it, take it inside her and make it tell. The trail traces over it. It knows the prey. It can tell. It can tell.

Its head moved. Looking.

Lips moving. Telling her. Cum shit piss dripping down it.

"The Bucket."

What?

I don't understand. These things, their world, anything. We moved and curled through our eternities. We raised palaces of our flesh, our filth, our love. We did not need cities, buildings, we were all the world, everything in the world was of us, the world was our need our glory of ourselves we did not have these walls these things. We did not need almost to speak. Its head jerked, its arms flailing. "The Bucket... Tash... I don't know..."

It was pointing back the way it had come. Jerking. Dead arm bones flapping dead skin. Kill it. Enjoy it.

She let it go, dropped it. It fell and flapped, croaking. Gasped for breath.

"Nothing," she hissed in her own voice. "Nothing happened here." Shimmer around it. The air cold and hot. It staggered up on legs as heavy as her own. Reeled and stumbled, blinked. Straightened. Stared around it. Not seeing her. Its head twisted back and forth. Set strong. It walked out away from her with the city shuddering ruin. Strong and steady, confident of itself, swinging the weapon at its hip.

Nothing.

Iananr turned the way it had been pointing. The alley she had found it in. And beside that… Windows. Lights. A doorway. Bustling, buzzing, talking, laughter, singing. The door opened, light showed, a smell of meat cooking, a voice shouted for more drink. A party of people in the street approached: two women arguing, a man with a third woman on its arm, pawing at it, it giggled and wriggled back.

An inn.

Another doorway, in the alleyway. Just near where the two men she had followed had stood to piss. The confusion of their trails, and its trail, the prey's trail, and the piss-stink, and the women still lying there, its grey head in the men's trickling piss. Iananr watched.

There. The man had pointed there. She took a few steps towards it. The walls and the doors of the inn shook, the army outside loosing something that made the city walls tremble. She could feel the dust of it. Taste the dust. Taste the soldiers up there shaking. In her real eyes she saw the soldiers swimming in petty magics, thrashing, shrieking.

The alley door opened, a man stared out into the street wiping its hands on its clothes. Big and heavy. Greasy grey smears on its hands. Dead flesh beneath its fingernails. Looked out towards the city walls and sighed.

"Gods, gods, help us," it muttered to itself.

"We're running out of lamp oil," a voice shouted to it.

"Then they'll have to drink in the dark," it shouted back. "If we're any of us still alive by then."

Calm, on the surface. Thrashing terror beneath, choked down. But calm, on the surface, in both of them. Almost becoming used to this. Unreal. Just another normal thing.

"Do you know?" it shouted back to the other voice, "we've made more money in the weeks since the Tsarii came than we have in the last three months?"

Two soldiers went past her towards the city walls filthy with sweat and ashes, grey with fatigue. One's arm was bandaged. Iananr stood waiting. The wounded man reeked of grief and bitterness. Wanted to go back to being a soldier. The other man reeked of grief and bitterness. Wanted to go back to being a man of peace. Pleasure hate drifted warm over her. Taste of their rage at dying. Sweet. Heat in her crotch, mounting in her. Writhe in it. Sink into it. Maggot pleasure burrowing into their death-grief. Once her kind ruled all this world, breathed in these agonies, we bent these filth-creatures to us. For eternities, we sank into their pain and their shame and their sorrow, opened ourselves into them. We swam in their deaths. Taste it. Smell it. The army outside the walls. The people gathered here waiting. All the shadows of their dying. Such pleasure she has not felt for so long.

Her master: "When the Tsarii come, Iananr, if you are good, I might let you wander. Loosen the chain a little while. Yes?"

People coming in and out of the inn doorway. Talking. Laughing. Sighing. Hopeful terrified resigned to their deaths. Sweetness of murderers, killers, fighters, liars; desperate broken bodies; hearts running with hate and fear and love. Soar on wings of their pain. Crawl in mounds of their decay. Hot pleasure, rippling over her. Glut herself. Gorge herself. Sink herself into their deaths. It reeked of dying. It sang of dying. It shimmered with putrid death rot. Let me love you, let me touch you, let me be you. Whole landscapes of pain in their hot dying breath. A woman praying with every breath for its lover's life. A man longing to die fighting, after things it has done it tried not to accept about itself.

But not the prey. It won't come here. It's fleeing you. It's escaped. Stab of self-loathing. It escaped me. Such shame.

Find it.

Soldiers up there on the walls, dying. Soldiers in the lines beyond, the besiegers, dying of boredom and disease. She hid herself in the dirt, screamed in her own tongue in her own mind with frustration and need and rage.

Find it. Word-chains making her ache with grief. Find it. Kill it.

Scent trails. Something moving. Footsteps.

Hope. Pitiful, in one such as her kind.

A name in the air, a word, a knowing.

Tash.

The inn door opening. Warm and noise. A voice shouting for another drink. A woman's loud laugh.

It's here. It's gone inside.

The prey.

Find it. Kill it.

Iananr pushed the door open and went in.

CHAPTER THREE

NOTHING ELSE IN HIS
LIFE BUT THIS

DESPERATION STINKS, THOUGHT Pitt, sitting in the back corner of The Dripping Bucket. Or maybe it was the spilled beer, puddled puke, the waft of urine sweeping in every time someone opened the back door to pee in the alley, or the fact that fat bastard Katch had once again burned whatever he was cooking. Which smelled suspiciously like hair.

Fucking skin the dog before you cook it.

He checked the front door. Nothing. No sign of Tash. The tit was probably dead anyway. No, calm down, the tit wasn't due for another hour or more.

Pitt lifted his pint, found it empty, and returned it to the table with a sigh.

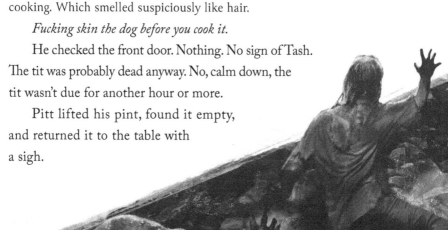

Two women sat with him. Normally that would have been cause for some excitement, but one was Gertri, the squad's Shield, and the other was Lashiahar, the enemy.

Pitt darted a quick glance. Face isn't bad. A little pinched. If she smiled… Remembering the last time some Watchman told Feylash she should smile more often, he stifled a grin with a cough. Yeah. Keep that stupid shit to himself. Something about the way Lashiahar moved made him think she'd be mean with a short-blade.

"Does it smell like someone is trying to cook an unskinned cat?" asked Lashiahar, petite nose wrinkling. She spoke with no hint of a Tsarii accent.

"Dog," grunted Gertri.

Whereas Gertri was large-boned and strong, built like a cross between a moose and a rabid bulldog, Lashiahar was small and lean. If the Tsarii spy possessed curves of any sort, those layers of mud-brown, tattered leather armour ill-concealed beneath a stained cloak, hid them masterfully.

Lashiahar scowled at the crowd, clearly uncomfortable with being in such close quarters with a room full of sweaty, drunken soldiers. "You Sharaami boil most things to a tasteless mush and burn everything else black."

"Burnt bits are the best," said Gertri, watching the front door, hand moving toward her knife as Casey stumbled in. The drunk staggered to his usual table and she relaxed. Somewhat.

"I prefer the mushy bits," said Pitt.

Gertri snorted. "Same way he likes his women."

"Gertri," said Lashiahar. "Feylash. Wint." Turning to Pitt she asked, "Why is your team all women?"

Pitt shrugged. "The team used to be mostly men, but they all died."

She didn't know about Anukat, the Axe. It was always a good idea to keep a little something in reserve. Or, in Anukat's case, a big something.

"Pfshh!" said Gertri. "He just likes to surround himself with pretty things."

Letting that slide, Lashiahar asked, "Where is this assassin of yours?"

"He'll be here," said Pitt.

"And he'll do better than the last two?"

Unfuckinglikely. "He is very good." At mooning over unavailable women and knifing small-time thieves no one gives a fuck about.

"You called him the third-best assassin in Sharaam," said Lashiahar.

"To drive his price down." Smothering a grin, Pitt remembered the boy's face, the look of stung hurt. If anything, I was generous. That panty-stain wasn't even top ten.

The front door swung open again and Anukat entered, ducking his head so as not to crack his skull on the transom. Mud and blood rained from his beard to join the growing mess on his chest. Leather armour stretched tight across his huge frame. The remnants of a rusted chain hauberk hung in tatters, sewn crudely to the leather. The big man rubbed at the Anakanari tribal scars ridging his face, making a show of scanning the room. Ice-blue eyes slid past Pitt with no hint of recognition. A tavern full of hard-bastard drunken soldiers, criminals and nutters so lacking in self-preservation skills they regularly ate the food served here, and everyone avoided eye contact, pretended not to see him.

Blood in his beard? Wait, did he bite someone's ear off again?

Scowling in disappointment, Anukat spun and exited the tavern, the door slamming behind him.

After counting to three hundred, Pitt said, "Gotta piss," and pushed to his feet.

"Have fun," Gertri said.

Ignoring her, Pitt headed out the rear door and into the alley. If The Dripping Bucket stank of urine, the alley was a thousand times worse.

Deciding he had to pee after all, he headed to the wall.

Anukat sauntered up beside him. Hauling out that war-hammer of a cock, he unleashed a torrent of urine that would leave a warhorse with a crushing inferiority complex.

"Do you have to do that now?"

"Sorry, boss," said Anukat. "This way it looks like we're having a friendly slash rather than whispering secrets in a piss-alley."

Pitt glanced meaningfully up and down the empty alley, but Anukat was too busy to notice.

A writhing ball of twisting green flame screamed past overhead to land somewhere in the north end of the city. Those were the worst. Even the rain struggled to put out that green fire.

"What's the word?"

"Bad," grunted the big Anakanari.

Oh hell. "How bad?"

Anukat turned his scarred face up to the rain to let it wash some of the blood from that ragged mop of beard. He spat. "We're dead."

"Oh. Fuck." Tash failed. What now? Grab Lashiahar and force her to take Pitt and his team with her when she left? "What did you see?" Anukat had been hiding outside the palace.

"Moments after entering the palace, Tash fled. Jumped right off the balcony. Ran away like the very gates of Kanar opened behind him."

Tash was still alive? "Why?"

Anukat shrugged. "A serving girl, a little fat lump of a thing, came out onto the balcony after he left. Must have startled him."

Oh, for fuck's fuck's fuck's sweet fucking sake.

Pitt's mind raced. "We have to act fast. You find Feylash. I'll find Wint." The Shroud was searching the buildings along the wall in case Lashiahar had people working on tunnelling. Gods alone knew where Feylash was. "We'll meet back here."

With a quick nod, Anukat took off at a jog, disappearing into the night.

Forgot to ask him about the blood.

Ducking back into The Dripping Bucket, Pitt returned to the table but didn't sit.

"I just got word that King Inshiil is dead," he lied. "Gertri, you wait here for Tash." Pitt prayed that if the assassin showed up, he'd be smart enough to play along.

Gertri grunted.

"Lashiahar," he continued, "it's probably best if you come with me." *I don't want you anywhere I can't lay a blade against your throat as the first step in negotiating our escape.*

"And where are we going?" she asked.

"To confirm the truth of the situation and, assuming Inshiil is truly dead, gather the team."

"How exciting." Reaching for her whiskey, she finished it in a slow swallow, examined the empty tin cup, turning it in artist's fingers, and carefully placed it back on the table.

Pitt stared at the cup. Something… Something in the way she set it down. Too careful, too deliberate. It was like the way his wife tidied their home before the Cvalene took her for cleansing.

She knew she would never return.

She knew she was going to die.

That was when he knew that Lashiahar had lied. There was no escape from this doomed city. Not even for her.

She's going to die here with us.

* * *

WELL, THAT WAS about as subtle as an enormously unsubtle thing. Got to love that about blokes—the way they always thought going for a slash was any kind of cover for anything.

Unless… woah, fuck… unless they really did. "Just going for a piss suddenly, rubbish bladder control, me, the draft when the big guy in armour I've never seen before and am avoiding eye-contact with so avidly you'd have to conclude he caught me humping his cat last night, when he opened the door the draft went straight to my bladder, I need a piss urgently, excuse me."

"Oh, I know, I know. Always happens to me too."

Which meant… they, like, really thought two women going for a slash together were just going for a slash?

Gertri the Shield, hardest of the hard, toughest of the tough, seen it all, killed it all, slept like a baby through her next-door neighbour's house literally blowing up a few days ago. But some things are too horrifying to think about.

Gertri took a long sip of her beer. Anyway.

So the king's dead. We have achieved it. The mission has been pulled off. Woop.

Take a quick look round: nothing's changed or will change. The shrieks will start from somewhere, no matter how clever they try to be in the castle about keeping it all secret so as not to frighten the cowered masses. The city'll roll over and the enemy troops will march in. Best we get out, then, pronto. I mean… if I'd hired someone to kill the king, I know what I'd be thinking about doing next. And it wouldn't be coughing up a pile of cash and a magic exit. Gertri wondered sometimes if Pitt had guessed what the reward Lashiahar had promised them actually was. 'Out of the war?' Oh yes.

He must have. She took another sip of beer. Watched the door still swinging from Pitt and Lashiahar walking out. Must have.

Odd feeling, having pulled it off.

So now when Tash turned up she'd need to say something like "Congratulations on your first successful regicide." Possibly buy him a drink and a bowl of dog-meat, find a way to get him outside and stick her knife in his gut.

Not the drink and the bowl of dog meat first, she thought then. Gross, if that came back out.

Ran her fingers over the knife hilt. She assumed she'd have to kill Tash. Pitt had never actually strictly speaking said so, but… Obviously the obvious thing to do. Even if Pitt was a bloke who thought "I'm just going for a slash" was subtle. The look he'd given her when he walked out, that… edgy look. "Wait here for Tash," with a note in his voice as he said it. Meant: "Wait here to kill Tash." Yes?

What else am I supposed to do with a bloke who just killed our king? Our king, man! We might have set it up for him to do it, salivated over the money we were creaming off his fee, but… he killed our king. Not something people should be boasting about. Insulting to the whole city, somebody killing our king.

The walls of the Bucket shuddered as an explosion hit somewhere nearby. Tsarii lobbing stuff at them day and night now. There was plaster dust in her beer. "How long we going to keep holding out?" one of the drinkers shouted. "We should surrender. This is insane. We should give up."

Someone else yelled back, "We're never going to give up! We'll win! Win!" Two of the off-duty soldiers were on their feet looking furious. Even Casey the drunk looked up, stared around at the soldiers, blinked.

Bar fight! Only form of entertainment left when your city's about to fall to an enemy army and the fuckers have blown up the playhouse, the dancing hall, and the market. Even started targeting the brothels recently, which might be the death-knell to the nobles' intentions to hold out. If they ever hit the Bucket or the Dying Poet… Gertri shuddered to think. She sat back having a quick look. Kind of nice to see people flexing their muscles. They were all so cooped up in this damned place. She was looking forward to killing Tash, actually. Use her own muscles a bit. Stretch her arms and legs.

Bar fight? Nope. Buggers sat down again, made up from wanting to kill each other, went back to talking about how good it was going to be killing Tsarii when they, uh, came screaming howling through the city walls with swords and axes and knives and knuckles and teeth.

And, oh ye gods and little fishes, that git Acol was starting up talking, and An and Flet were starting up talking, and someone better not be about to sing that obsidian hearts song again…

Be nice to kill that Tsarii cow who'd hired them actually, though. That could be a good-fun fight. She'd be a great opponent, fast and clever to Gertri's thick muscle. Test her a bit, rather than sitting around on her arse barely able to go for a walk, in case a siege weapon went off. "Are all your team women?" Oh, yes, we girls do love following a big strong man around. He explains things to us, tells us what we should be doing, takes us girls on out of the kindness of his gentlemanly heart. Or possibly he takes on the best and the best just happened to be women in some cases, Ms Get-Me-I'm-So-Special-Cause-I'm-A-Soldier-With-Tits. Don't know about the Tsarii, but here in dog-eating Sharaam, women warriors aren't anything to make a thing about. And if he's running the show and I'm not, that's because I've got three kids and a house and a husband I need to think about occasionally, while Pitt, sad fuck that he is, he's got nothing else in his life but this.

The Bucket shook again. More plaster in the dregs of Gertri's beer. If Lashish-what's-her-face didn't have the only way to get those three kids and maybe the husband out of this place before it falls and we all get butchered, I'd kill her.

Screams, somewhere distant outside. A building must have come down again. Bane fire toasting someone. And Tash walked in.

Fucker looked around like he was hoping Pitt'd be there. Congratulations, man, you just totally fucked over your own city! Have a beer!

Right, so, let's do this: Gertri put her hand on her sword hilt. An assassin's assassin. Niche job role, that.

Pitt does mean me to kill Tash. Doesn't he?

Occurred to her she should maybe have double-checked…

Tash was bending over Casey the drunk, talking.

Tash looked… a bit odd, it occurred to Gertri. Not exactly what you'd call triumphant. More like he was about to be sick.

She shrugged. Make it easier to kill him.

I really should have checked if I was supposed to kill him. Pitt's a decent leader but a rubbish manager. This is where a project plan would have been of use.

When in doubt, kill him. Easier to sort out if it turned out not to have been the right thing to do.

Sidle up to him. Ready, steady… Right, third-best assassin… ready to die? Go in with a nudge, tip her beer down herself, knife him one. "He spilled my pint, your honour. It was all completely justified, no court in the land could convict me."

He was looking even sicker. Like… I'm going to throw up right now sick.

Useful, if he started puking. She could help him outside into a dark alley, everyone knew she was good with puke, what with having three kids.

Ready. Steady…

And now Tash was talking to some girl. For fuck's sweet sake. Couldn't people just leave him alone to be killed easily? The girl had a thing for him, it reeked off her. Poor love. Neither of them exactly spoiling a pair. But a bit harsh, maybe, doing Tash in in front of his girl.

And then.

The door opened, and a woman came into the Bucket. Mushy. Like Pitt didn't like his women. Fat lumpy little thing. Gods, terrible dress sense. *You'd look so much better if you cut your hair, belted your dress; that colour really doesn't work on you.* That was what Gertri should think, looking at her. Mousy woman with bad dress sense. Barely notice, except…

A smell. That was the thing. A rank smell, rank even over the smell of the Bucket. Not strong—subtle, like she might be imagining it, only she wasn't imagining it because she felt sick to her stomach like she'd discovered the meat she was eating was maggot-ridden, Gertri's skin crawling, but so subtle she must be imagining it. Ghost of a smell, like one of kids saying "wet fart" in the middle of a family meal.

Fucking fuck.

I know that smell.

Run. Just run…

The woman raised her head like she was sniffing the air. Pale eyes. Pale face. Opened her mouth a crack. Nervous high laugh from a server with a pint mug. Mad brain-dead confusion: this little dumpy mouse thing you wouldn't look twice at, and you're somehow soiling yourself because it feels so wrong and she's… she's… wrong.

Triumph for women, yeah, Gertri thought somewhere as the woman came nearer, mouth open. Always the quiet shy ones.

Pale eyes locked onto Casey sitting at the next table. Lips curled, mouth open, sniffing. Gertri was going to be sick. Casey was going to be sick.

Casey the drunk was bleeding. Blood running down him. Blood everywhere. And the blood… Like it's alive. Like Casey was all just maggots inside him. Maggots: just pouring out of him.

Like when Gertri's youngest had worms. And the worms were in her youngest's shit.

Lanterns go out. It's morning. It's black as night.

Silence.

* * *

Pitt set a hard pace toward the walls and Lashiahar walked at his side like they were out for a gentle stroll. His mind reeled, thoughts stumbling in a mad panic. *I imagined that.* No way this spy planned on dying here. No fucking way. She had to have a way out. Wint would get it out of her. This Tsarii spy had no idea. The Shroud would peel her like a three-year-old peeling an orange. A sticky fucking mess with strands of weird fibrous stuff tangled around fingers and fruit guts littered all over the table. Glee and bright eyes and a sloppy—*Doesn't Gertri have a three-year-old? When was the last time I had an orange? Snap out of it!*

Either Lashiahar had a way out of the doomed city, or Pitt would find one. Make one. Whatever.

Yeah. Right. The whole fucking city wants to escape but I'm the special one who gets his people out.

Even the buildings, leaning as if straining against their foundations, looked like they were getting ready to leave. Crossing a main thoroughfare, the sounds of fighting at the wall, the crash and crush of murder on a mass scale, echoed down the empty street. Sharaaam cowered, hid in basements, sat slumped in pubs and taverns, drank the last scummed dregs of the cheapest spirits.

What if he abandoned his team? Sure as shit would be easier to get out alone. No way Gertri would leave the kids behind. The husband—useless fuck-waffle—gods, you could never tell what she felt about him. One day she talked about using his guts to hang her laundry—*does she really do laundry?*—and the next she gushed on about how great he was with the kids.

If he got out alone, Anukat's long-dead ancestors would hunt him down, Wint would look at him with those eyes, and Feylash…

Idiot.

Maybe he had a soft spot for the Knife. Exactly the kind of spot she'd put one of those blades if he even thought about abandoning her. *Stupid to have a soft spot for something so hard, so lacking in soft spots.* At least Gertri hadn't noticed. Gods and demons, he'd never hear the end of it if she realised he was soft on Feylash. Or was it hard?

Focus!

It was all lies and incontinent donkey shite anyway. No way he'd leave his team behind. Too long. Too much history.

Fine. So, he'd get them all out. Hell, maybe he'd even save Lashiahar. He glanced at the spy. *No. Fuck it. She dies here. Deserves it for lying to us.*

Something flitted across the sky in jumpy fits and starts, twitching back and forth, side to side, in a way unnatural to the rules of the world. It shuddered, shedding shivering globs of writhing purple-green that grew limbs as they fell, becoming tentacled monstrosities or maybe spiders with too many legs and eyes. They screamed as they plummeted to the earth. Terrible sound. Fear and rage.

"The fuck are those?" he demanded, slowing, as one dropped in the direction they were heading.

"Alchemical creations. Short-lived. Soul-sparks of the tortured dead bound to—"

"Shut up! Shutup shutup shutup! Some. Things. I. Don't. Want. To. Know."

"Where we going?" asked Lashiahar.

"To find Wint."

"Wint?"

"The Shroud."

"Shrouds are real?" she asked, voice all doubt.

"They are."

"Where is she?"

"No idea."

Lashiahar stopped, and Pitt stopped too, though he wasn't sure why he was keeping her with him. Stupid blind hope he was wrong about her not having a way out? Hell, might as well keep her until he knew she was useless.

"Then how are we going to find her?" the Tsarii spy asked. "You seem to be running in random directions."

Of course he was. Searching was pointless, a waste of time. "She'll find me. She always does. But it only works if I look for her first." *And only if she wants to find me.*

The Shroud could be gone already. Maybe she had her own way out of the city. Maybe—

Wrapped tight in rotting gauze, shrouded from head to toe in wisps of acrid mist and decaying cotton, there but not there, Wint stepped from the shadows. Only those eyes, bright and mad, were exposed to the world. Only the eyes were real. Anukat said that if you peeled away those endless layers of fabric, you'd find nothing but crazy eyes floating in smoke. Pitt didn't even know why he referred to Wint as female. The ethereal twisting material, floating about her like she was sinking in the ocean, hinted at hidden curves. That and the voice, rich like silk, warm like melting butter. Gertri once said she'd fuck Wint for the voice alone. Of course she also went on about the Shroud's hilarious sense of humour.

"Fucking—" barked a startled Lashiahar, flinching away from the Shroud.

Pitt nodded greeting. "We have to find Anukat and Feylash."

Ice-shard eyes. Smoke and soul. "The king sent a demon after Tash."

Well fuck. Good job on the subtlety and not spilling potentially dangerous information to the enemy. Was that supposed to be funny? Was this her 'hilarious sense of humour' at work?

"King Inshiil isn't dead?" demanded Lashiahar. "You lied?" She sounded hurt, like, if you can't trust hired murderers, who the hell can you trust?

"Not like you were ever going to pay us," said Pitt, turning on the spy. "Not like you were ever going to get us out."

Painted in guilt, she looked away. "There was… supposed to be… I only found out this morning. Expendable."

She hadn't known. So fucking what. She was the enemy anyway. He should kill her. Right now. Sword in the guts. Leave her to bleed out, retching and sobbing in the street.

Razor eyes watched the exchange, wisps of fabric wafting about the Shroud even though there was no hint of a breeze. "Tash is going to The Dripping Bucket."

The Shroud's words sank in. Inshiil sent a demon after Tash. Tash going to the Bucket. Gertri at the Bucket waiting for Tash.

"Fuck."

Not the end of the world. They'd killed demons before. As a team. No one fought a demon, not even a minor Ashen, alone.

What if it wasn't an Ashen? Why did King Inshiil have a demon? What else did he have hidden away? Was the city less doomed than Pitt thought? A score of tracers spitting alchemical fire arced across the sky, wrote lines on Pitt's pupils, purple after-images of death, and fell in the Church District. The ground shook, and the Cvalene Cathedral crumpled in on itself like a deflating pig's bladder.

Nope. King Inshiil had nothing. One demon wasn't going to save the city.

"We have to get back to the Bucket," said Pitt. "Gertri—"

"Stink-rot. Putrescence," said Wint. "Feylash softly, softly. Slowly Anukat. Needs: to the vessel."

The Shroud hated pubs, said they smelled like dying futures, whatever that meant. But she was right. They needed the whole team. Or at least that's what he thought she said. One could never be too sure.

As for: *softy softly* … he didn't have time to think about it. Feylash had been a bit off with him recently, mind. Maybe Wint meant he should … buy her some flowers or something? Have a friendly chat?

What? Pitt shook his head. *Focus, man. I think I might be going into shock.*

"Time is death," said Wint.

Was this the humour Gertri was always on about?

No, she means we don't have time. Probably.

"Back to the Bucket," Pitt decided. "We have to get Gertri."

Lashiahar touched his arm.

"What?" he snapped.

"There's still a way," she said, voice small. "Kill King Inshiil and I can get you out." She swallowed, licked her lips. "Maybe."

Pitt stared at her. Maybe. The cup of whiskey. The way she'd looked at it. The way she'd set it so carefully on the table. "You're lying."

Lashiahar shrugged, said nothing.

"Wint will get it out of you."

"Shit soul," said the Shroud. "Flayed."

"Do you have time for that?" the spy asked.

After. After they got Gertri.

"Death time soul stink," said Wint.

Death time indeed.

Pitt ran for The Dripping Bucket and the spy and the Shroud followed.

* * *

A LIGHT. KATCH the innkeep lighting a candle. "What the fuck?" Katch's voice. "What the fuck—"

Katch just opened up. Right there. Head to arsehole, fucking split in half. His lips moved. Both sides of them. He was still just about alive as he fell down left and right. His hands even jerked, like he was trying to reach and hold onto himself. Flickering in the candle-light.

Nervous high laugh. Someone shat themselves, someone pissed themselves, someone started crying for their mum.

All the bits of Katch exploded. Red-black-white-pink-brown spatter on the walls, on everyone there. Stinging. Flesh and fat and bone and innards, hard and painful as shrapnel for a war machine. Gertri felt it cut her face.

"Not it," the mousey woman said.

Turned to face Gertri. Sniffed at her.

"You?"

Everything smells of decay. Rot stink. Menstrual blood congealing on shit-soiled rags. Can't run. Can't move.

"You?" the mousey woman said. "Where is it? Where is it?"

She could see its real face. Gods. Writhing. Can't see it. Right up in front of her and she can't, can't, can't. Long black tongue came out, forked towards Gertri's mouth. "Where is it?"

I ... I ... uh—

The server with the pint mug moved. Gods know why. Maybe her body simply gave up and collapsed in fright. Crumpled, jerked, shat herself, black blood pooling between her thighs.

Fuck.

Mum, Gertri found herself thinking.

Rot stink right up in Gertri's face. Can't see it.

"It escaped me. Escaped me. Where is it?"

Demon.

Fuckfuckfuckfuckfuckfuckfuckfuckfuckfuckfuck.

Teeth in her face. Fuck. Screaming everywhere everywhere like they're all all fucking dead.

The table she was sitting at exploded.

"Where is it?" the thing screamed.

Demon. It's a fucking demon.

Gertri stuttered out, "I don't... don't... don't..." Going to vomit from the stench. Her body hurt worse than childbirth. More terrified than anything. Fought a demon you've fought a demon you can survive you—

"Tell!" it screamed.

Not thinking not seeing, outside herself watching this happening. Fuckfuckfuckfuck. *Fought a demon—You fought—My children, irritating little shitheads, the three of them, my meathead husband I'm stuck with because the children, oh gods, oh sweet mercy, my children. Never been so scared in war or on any job, ever. I'm the Shield. I don't do this alone. The Shield, the Axe, the Knife, the Shroud. Not alone.*

Gertri's hand on her sword hilt. Knew it was useless. The sword blade was swinging between her and the demon. She hit it and she felt it. The blade grated against its arms. Rasped with a sound like fingernails. Felt weak in Gertri's hand, like the sword had gone in, cut down. Easy killing, easy as cutting down children that time in Ailnoug when she was a soldier, when they were the besiegers, when they took a city and went in and killed everyone. She should have killed it, if it had been a person. She felt the sword cut it down and she heard the sword rasp against it like she was trying to cut stone.

"Where is it?"

"I don't... don't... don't..." *Mummy. My pissing burden on my life children. No.*

It was looking for something she knew.

Tash. Gertri's eyes slid to the door, where Pitt had left with the spy who said she could get her children out of here.

"Tash..."

He'd gone.

"Find it," the demon hissed. Green foam on its bloody lips. It saw where Gertri was looking. "There. Is that it? Is that it?"

Pitt: in the doorway. *There's the woman who said she can get her children out of here. There's the Shroud, Wint. Gods. Thank you. As a team, we can do this. We've done it before, killed a demon, we—*

We—

Too late.

Green foam burned on Gertri's face and hands. *Fuckfuckfuckfuck-fuckfuckfuckfuckfuck. My pissing pox on them burden children, please, gods.*

A thousand rows of teeth closed on her.

She sees it as it really is as she dies inside it. Dying inside it is a relief.

Voices are screaming: "Gertri! Fucking Gertri!" "What the fuck are you doing? Are you insane?" "Stink-rot. Pus. Purge. It killed Gertri." "Are you insane?"

They come through the inn doors, Pitt and Wint and the spy who can save Gertri's children. Pitt draws his sword and Wint the Shroud crackles out black light. Half the inn's got swords out, running at it, screaming at it. Watch. Soldiers. Cut-throats. Kill it! Scared! So: kill! Half the inn's running away, howling, screaming, shitting, puking blood.

The spy is shouting, "What the fuck are you doing? Run!"

"It killed Gertri," Wint the Shroud whispers. Black light cracks over it. Lights it up. White eyes in a black skull. It turns, shrieking. Lets go of whatever's left of Gertri's self. It gasps at Wint. Its mouth moves and moans. Gertri's sword is hanging out of its arm. Blood spraying. The metal hissing. The steel melting away into its arm. The red glass in the end of Gertri's sword that she's so proud of winks at it.

"Are you insane?" the spy screams. "Run."

A thousand mouths. A thousand clawed hands. It stinks like dead meat. It reaches for Wint. Black light envelopes it. Rolls over it. Curling and soft, like a woman swaddling a corpse in a grave-sheet. It shakes itself. Twists and writhes. Shrieks like it's trapped. Its claws rip the air. Thin woman's arms, flabby underneath, dry cracked skin at the elbows, dirt smears on the skin. The light crumples off it. It bares its teeth. Swordsmen rush at it. Pitt, the idiot, rushes at it.

Wint's shrouded form flickers. For a moment, in her white pain haze, Gertri thinks she can see Wint's face.

Wint is …

… is …

The walls of the Bucket rock and plaster falls from the ceiling, the Tsarii blowing up the city around them as they fight.

Gertri can see everything dying.

Dying inside it is a relief.

CHAPTER FOUR

WE WALKED IN BLOOD

R UNNING IN THE pleasure, wet running grinding it in her teeth, close her lips over red softness ebbing enter in it red running, her teeth grin grinding bared closing. She gasps moving like axe blades her body opens holds it, closes, closes, the world is red her mouth her eyes her body red. Yields to it. Sinks in it. Iananr claws herself bites herself her body running loose sweet red.

The smell and the lights: this place is filled with people. And it's here, she knows. She can smell it. Its colours run through the air. So many colours, scent trails like streaming banners, all these beautiful shin-ing people here. She can go through them kill them kill all of them. Kill ev-erything.

This thing here stinks of her prey. Colour trails swirl off it. She's confused, because the scent trails mix, bleeding together like the light's edge, looking and staring at something so long the colours are changed. Her body's eyes say that this one looks different. Not the prey she seeks for. It has the prey scent and it has another scent on it, like blood merging into salt water.

This place is confusing to her. Too many people close here together, all of it merging, the prey smells of them, the human smells she can sense with this body's revulsion. She in this false trapping body smells like them. The stink of them overwhelms her. Vile and rich. So pleasant. But this man has the prey scent spiralling over it, and she holds out her arms to it and pulls it into her. It yields into her almost too easy. She grasps it her hands tearing, she enters it and it enters her she chokes biting into it, the pleasure beats in her its pleasure her pleasure, it moans into her and she croons to it with hot sweet pleasure love. But it comes down dead and empty and she thinks: that was not the prey. There's an emptiness there. The scent trails are blurred and wrong.

But: this man... knew her. She spits out the last of her pleasure over it. It knew her, she had known it before. Her master, the one who bound her here, set her seeking this thing also. It was trying to take something important. She cannot understand this importance placed on objects. Her master had bound her to punish for the theft of an object. This is the man here, flesh lump sinking away fading nothing left but the feel of its death in her body.

She thinks a human word: thief.

How very foolish. A sweetness, because her master will be pleased and in gratitude her master will not tighten her chains. And she thinks again: we were the rulers of all. We walked in blood and they knelt to us screaming, we walked on landscapes of their bodies' suffering, their songs of love for us rang out. Now I am come to this: I fear them because they can hurt me.

Sweetness, I feel, because I have done something to please the one who bound me. She thinks: what have I become? What am I reduced to? I will turn on my master and make it suffer and make it scream and die and wallow in its pain, and it—

The chains jerk tight into her, ripping at her. Her master's words, smiling into her: 'You are bound, Iananr, you are tied tight into these word-chains; they will hurt you in ways you cannot feel beyond suffering. They will make you feel as men feel, Iananr.' This is how they feel, then. This is how... the man she has killed felt.

It stole an object of value and she has killed it. Punishment.

She turns from it threading her way through this chaos. They're all staring at her. All afraid. She looks, searching, the scent trails are here, the knowledge of what she is seeking is here, taste it, feel it. She shifts, turns, seeking.

A woman, the woman knows things. She can see the prey's scent on it, staining it bright like it's been dipped in water. She comes at it and she thinks—oddly, briefly—of the little girl she met and spared, for there is the same shape and scent of something there in the woman's mind.

"Where is it?"

Her tongue fumbles over the sounds.

"Where is it?"

Is she speaking the wrong language? Trapped in here she cannot remember sometimes how to speak to these people, who used once to sing to her in their fear and their cravings, understood her without the need for her to speak.

"Find it." Teeters, trying to make the words, pain hunger choking her, pleasure so she can't remember how to speak. The woman's head turns, its eyes moving, looking. Iananr whispers screams, "There. Is that it? Is that it?" Find it.

The woman screams. It's beautiful. But it does not help her find anything. She feels the woman's rage, it's angry with her and she laughs and it fears her. Why are they all so frightened of dying? she thinks. Dying is… more of this.

Her hands and her mouth take the woman into her. It tastes too strongly of pain and regret. It tastes of love, this woman, love mixed with bitterness, a tired sad weary guilt. Iananr sinks herself into enjoyment. Its thoughts are filled with pity. The shape of its love for something is a stabbing discomfort, a sharp sudden lack of pleasure in Iananr's mouth. It is all worn down with something, dried out, and she does not enjoy it. There is regret, almost, for killing it. A bad taste in her, that its pleasure is distasteful.

No matter. It sinks away into dying. She pulls herself into it, sucks herself deep and cold into it. Its dying is her dying. Its pleasure grief in its death. 'Children,' its heart screams as she devours it. It feels regret and sorrow and guilt and peace all at once. She enjoys it, it enjoys it.

And a memory this woman had, swirling, fills her. She reels under it. Words. An image. The word-chains rip and stab at Iananr's mind, shrieking to her something deep and secret.

The king is dead, Iananr thinks. This woman she has killed: this woman knew that the king is dead. She hears the prey speaking. She can see its words, see the scene there as the woman saw it, the king dying. A sword stabbing into it, killing it.

The prey has killed it. Killed the king.

Her master: 'You will protect King Inshiil, Iananr. That is your one task. You are his guardian, you will keep him safe from all harm.' Her master's voice ripples, the word-chains gripping. 'Your one task.' Pulled away from her sleeping, soft, warm, wet dreams of all the worlds long gone. 'You are his guardian, Iananr. I bind you to him and I bind you to him. You shall not rest. You shall be kept here forever as a guard over him.'

Confusion mounts in her. She sees it, so clear: the woman listening, a man's voice saying bright, cheerful, nervous, 'I just got word that King Inshiil is dead.' The woman's feelings all mixed about it. Pleased. Surprised. Frightened. The man twitches. In the memory it looks… guilty? The woman wanted this and didn't want this and it's so clear in its mind, the man's voice, 'I just got word that King Inshiil is dead.' The woman gapes, half unbelieving, and then it believes.

Iananr screams. In her mind she sees King Inshiil, the thing she must guard. Solid tall meat-lump, proud: she laughed at how proud it was. It thought itself powerful like she is, thought it was different to the meat around it, better, stronger. 'The gods have blessed me. The gods have chosen me' it thought in its gold-crowned head. It was terrified of her, piss flaring between its legs as she stood there before it. But a thrill in it, she had tasted it, the thrill it felt that it was special enough that she was bound to guard it. She had felt it thinking on her as it spewed itself out into a woman. Calling on her. 'So special, so far above all others, I have a demon to guard me.' She had laughed at it, then. Pitied it its delusions. Later, once, it had spoken to her. Ordered her master to force her to crouch before it: 'Kiss the toe of my royal boot, demon. Master R'ylish, make the demon kneel. Make the demon say something.' A note of fear: 'Make the demon say something in praise of me.' And her master, looming over her: 'I bind you to him and I bind you to him. You shall not rest, you shall be kept here forever, keeping guard over him. That is all you are, demon. King Inshiil's guard.'

The prey is gone. Lost. She searches and she cannot find it.

'I just got word that King Inshiil is dead.'

Failure.

Rage.

Shame.

* * *

SHE OPENS THE tavern up into pieces. She is white and sick. The walls rock beneath her anger. The air inside is corroded, white poison, the drinkers' mouths open trying to breathe, gasping poison down into red lungs. Decay eats at them, healthy strong men tough with bright living. They breathe the air around her their bodies are corrupted, blood runs thick slow burning, the branches of their lungs wither, their bones begin to crumble. Iananr pulls them apart to show all the scars within them. They are sinking sinking sinking into death all around her. She takes her mouth to them, her heart, her strange unreal white hands. The walls of the tavern are wet with her pleasure. In this false human body her breath gasps pouring sweat onto the walls. The floor erupts beneath her, wave upon trembling wave.

She is within her own world, the surface of this human place is stretched thin to nothing, the word-chains pulled taut almost broken. Her shame and her failure lash across her and the tavern shakes in eddies of her pleasure. Waves. Tides. Her own body is taken apart by this. She gorges herself on and on. Blood and entrails, shit, bones, gristle. White brains spilling cream-soft, trampled by dying feet.

They are screaming, they are praising her glory in their screams. Desire overcomes them, they kneel to her, expose themselves, beg her for her touch. They thrash beneath her. She accepts their desire, their love. A man rushes at her, armed, a sword in its hand. She wrestles with it. Loving it. A woman rushes at her, filthy, wrapped in shadows. It delights her, she drops the man, turns to it. It has a bitter taste to it, she spits it out, rejects it. The tavern keeper falls towards her. Her human hands lift its body, caress it, her human tongue probes into its bowels licking it with corrosion, carving it, rending it, emptying it. The tavern keeper's wife is prostrate with worship, clutching at Iananr's body with heavy limbs flayed and crumbling. Iananr lays aside the husk of the tavern keeper, turns to the woman, rips it into fragments. Its bloodied arms embrace her. Passion leaks from it into

Iananr's mouth. A woman caparisoned in armour, the metal nuzzling her as she devours it. A thin frail boy with bruised arms, pulling itself into her with love. She shreds them. She dissolves them. Her human body and her real body probe the wounds she opens. She disjoints them. She severs them. She delights in them. Her fingers are knives. Her teeth. Her gaze. The air burns them. Their blood burns. The tavern walls soften into scar tissue. The tavern floor sucks the bodies down like lips. She kills, kills, kills, kills.

* * *

LIQUID DRIPS OVER grey stones. There is a void where the tavern the Bucket was standing. A gaping wide gash in the world, glistening, swollen up red-black.

She is almost sated. She wants to sleep.

'I just got word that King Inshiil is dead.'

She has failed. She feels… shame.

She thinks: that was… not a wise thing. The killer must be found, it has to be destroyed and her master might not punish her for her failure. How can this happen? 'Your one task.' Humiliation fills her. She is degraded by her failure. Her own thoughts debase her. Her master might not punish her! She has swum through eternities of human suffering, the abyss has opened at her touch, she has consumed stars and lives and souls. She grovels before her master, a slave. When I am free, she thinks, when I am free from these bindings I will…

She cannot think it. The bindings hold her ragged, block her mind. Her master is her master, she will be and do as her master bids her. Guard. Kill. Her master commands. Her master makes her what she is. Her master will punish her failure. She is bound, she does as she is bid.

But she would know. She is bound to the king, she is its guardian. She would know. She would be there, protecting it. What can have harmed it without her knowing? The king, hiding away in its castle, thick stone walls that even the one outside the walls with their siege weapons cannot break. How?

The prey, she thinks. The prey, the assassin that keeps escaping from her. It is... more powerful than she had understood. It has some ability to escape her, it fled from her to confuse her and it came back to kill the king. It can blind her. She cannot understand how. She thinks back, trying to picture it: the prey's fear of her, its confusion. It had felt weak and its scent trail was bitter with failure. 'The third best assassin': panic had flickered in it every time it thought that. It did not believe that. She had seen its horror of itself.

A disguise.

So what is it? If it can so trick and evade her?

Iananr thinks, with fear of her own: It is ... more powerful than I am. She feels... fear.

Fear. This creature ... monstrous ... Tash.

Fear him!

Voices outside in the street, coming closer:

"The whole place is destroyed."

"Fucking hells."

"Didn't see anything go over. Fuck, what have the Tsarii got to lob at us now?"

"Any survivors?"

"Any survivors? Fuck, man: any recognizable body parts?"

"It's all fucking wet! Wet and slimy, look, there's, like, mucus everywhere. What the fucking fuck?"

A woman's voice, "Looks like... Feels like... Reminds me of... It's..."

The woman's voice, "Never mind me, I must be sick in the head."

A figure bends down. "A woman's alive here! Cvani Lord of Light be praised! Are you alright, miss?"

The woman's voice: "A woman? She got her pants on... ? Never mind me, I must be sick in the head."

A hand reaches out to Iananr. A man is standing before her, concern all over its face. "Cvala Lady of Dark, you are a lucky woman. Can you stand? What happened?"

She can taste its kindness. For a moment she thinks: is this a disguise too? Is this another power summoned to trick me? What does this thing want? She thinks of fighting, destroying it. She is afraid. For a moment.

"I have to find it," she says in her human voice. She gets up. The man is wide-eyed. "Cnule Knave of Twilight, you're a lucky woman. Are you hurt?"

She looks at the man and it takes a step back. Remember how to speak. Remember. She says slowly, "I am not hurt."

It blinks. It... senses her. "I am not hurt," Iananr says again. "I am looking for someone. Tash," she says. "I am looking for man called Tash."

"What happened here?" the man asks. "An explosion? A Tsarii weapon?"

"Magery. Gods save us. Some kind of demon weapon," the woman says. "Whatever this was."

"The Tsarii are animals," a second man says. "What they've done here. Fucking deserves wiping out, the Tsarii army, for killing everyone here. Killing's too bloody good for them."

"Like..." A third man is inspecting the rubble, wiping his hands on grey stones, holds them up sticky, slimy, shining. It looks down at what was the floor of the tavern. "It does look like... Never mind."

"Tash," Iananr says again. Louder. "Tash. The third best assassin in Sharaam. Where? I am looking for it. Looking for him. And... Gert," she says. The name floats in her mind. Connected to Tash. Find Tash, find Gert, find... the dead woman's memory, cursing as it died... Iananr thinks: I must find ... Pitt.

But Tash is something powerful, to be feared. But Gert, she realizes then, is the woman she killed who knew the king was dead.

"Gert?" the woman says back to her. "Gert who ran with Pitt's crew? You know her?" The woman almost puts her hand on Iananr's arm. Draws its hand back puzzled, frightened, oblivious. Instinctive. "Was she here? Poor cow, I kind of hope she was. Her house was hit in the last bombardment. Her children are dead. I've been looking for her, to tell her before she goes home to it. I'm sorry," the woman says. "If you knew her."

Dead children? Yes. She remembers. From the woman Gert's mind as she died. Sated as she is, a feeling crawls through her. The woman loving its children but the children are already dead. A taste, a smell of love in Iananr's real mouth.

She thinks: if King Inshiil is dead, my purpose is to avenge the killing. If I am unsure what killed King Inshiil, then… then I will destroy… everything.

Failure. Rage. Shame.

She turns towards the people around her, digging in the swollen wound that was once the tavern the Bucket.

"Gods, look, here's… Ah fuck! Fuck fuck fuck fuck fuck fuck it's a fucking human hand a fucking hand fuck fuck fuck gods fuck."

"There's just… shreds. I mean… I mean…"

"I can't do this. I can't be here. I can't see this. Gods, let the Tsarii come and kill us all. I can't see this."

"What did the Tsarii do here?"

"What if the Tsarii do this again?"

"We should surrender. Gods, even that bastard Inshiil will have to surrender, when he sees this. We can't fight this."

Voices echo, pathetic, heartbroken, "We have to surrender now. We can't fight this."

The earth rocks again. The ones beyond the walls are beginning another barrage against the city. Somewhere far off, a trumpet sounds. And she feels… Something is happening. The city will fall soon. Power flickers in the air, in her world and in this absurd human place.

The ones beyond the walls? Something else?

She thought: the creature Tash. The 'third best assassin.'

She thought: but what purpose have I apart from killing, if King Inshiil is dead?

She thinks: what if my master is killed when the city falls? Will the bindings break? If the king is dead and her master dies and the chains do not break…

She thought then: this creature, Tash, that is so powerful he can escape her, kill without her knowing… If he is so powerful, could he help her? Break her bindings?

She thought, very clear, very certain: if the king is dead, and I have failed, what is it I am bound to? If not to the creature that killed him?

CHAPTER FIVE

A CITY SCREAMING

TASH RAN AND deadly silence followed with him.

No screams.

Dark. Black sky, all the light swallowed by suffocating blankets of cloud and smoke.

He splashed through a murky puddle. Sodden feet so cold they hurt, he ran faster.

Pale and bloody hells, screams would have been better than this bottomless silence.

Screams would mean that thing—that damned frumpy terrifying little woman—was still in the Bucket, killing everyone, ripping their insides out, making them bleed worms or whatever it did to Casey.

Writhing blood.

Seething blood.

Blood isn't supposed to fucking move! It just sits there pooling and maybe running downhill like any liquid!

What if she did it to me too?

What if that was why she let him go? What if, even now, his blood swam with swarms of twisting snakes?

Infected.

"Fuck!"

Daring a glance over his shoulder, Tash saw nothing but darkness. *That doesn't mean it isn't there.*

How had it found him?

Tash darted left into an alley and promptly tripped over what he thought was a corpse. It groaned, so he got up and ran harder, desperately struggling to puzzle out the lumpen shapes littering the ground. Feet slipping in mud, arms spread wide for balance, he dashed over something soft and squishy.

The southern horizon lit green and yellow as a spitting ball of fire arced over Sharaam, lighting the city in nauseous bile.

He slid to a stop to watch, hoping to gauge where it would land and find somewhere else to be. More fucking Tsarii alchemicals. Yet different. He hadn't seen one like this before. This was an exciting new shade of rot.

Finally going to end us with the big one?

The ball of fire slowed as it reached its apex and, impossibly, hung motionless in the sky like a second, sick sun. It was huge. Bigger and brighter. The city glowed puss. Every puddle. Every damp stone. Every inch of exposed flesh. The world shone bile.

Sharaam's new sun sat fat in the sky, an obese slug of squirming fire drooling molten horror upon the city. It spat and hissed and cracked.

A cancerous new day had dawned over the city, and it brought hell.

Tash heard the distant roar of the Tsarii troops as they charged the wall. This was it. The end. The walls would fall and the Tsarii would bring their vile gods to Sharaam. Maybe that hissing ball was their god. Knowing nothing of the Tsarii, he had no idea. It certainly seemed possible. Likely.

Pale and rotting hells, what is that stench?

The new sun?

Pulling his attention away, Tash looked around the now green-lit alley.

Corpses.

Corpses everywhere. Underfoot. Hanging from windows, split and littered across the street. The locals must have been tossing their dead into this alley since the siege began.

Not mud. Tash stood ankle-deep in gore. A loop of glistening intestine twisted around one foot like a bloated snake.

One corpse raised a hand, reaching weakly. Imploring.

Then another.

Not dead?

Hundreds of milky, rotten eyes locked on him. They spoke as one voice, the word unknowable.

Tash's mind refused to even attempt to parse the meaning.

One thought: *Run, you stupid fucker.*

He didn't move. Couldn't. Too many eyes.

A ripple ran through the corpses, built into a surging wave. Clambering flesh. They were one. Moved as one. Spoke as one.

That word.

It murdered thought. Strangled hope.

For a mad instant, Tash imagined an angry child bashing open a boiled egg with a spoon and clumsily digging out the yolk, only the egg was his skull.

And then he was on his knees, slick intestines curling around his legs, tightening. Endless coils of constricting gut snaking through the gore, searching, questing.

Run. Stupid. Fucker.

Mass graves, much like this one, littered Sharaam. How many dead were piled at the city gate? Too tired to cart away the corpses, the soldiers had been tossing them over the wall. Let the enemy deal with them, Tash guessed.

Thousands. Tens of thousands of corpses.

All Sharaam's dead.

Another sound grew, echoed off stone. Screams of terror and panic. A city screaming.

Cowering from reality, some part of Tash's brain fled to math, seeking escape in the comprehensible mundane. There'd been maybe one and a half million people in Sharaam before the war. Surprisingly few fled, most failing to understand the severity of the threat. At least a million souls still cowered within the city walls. What percentage of that number had died? Ten percent? Tash suspected it was closer to thirty but was unwilling to face the thought of three hundred thousand living corpses. And how many Tsarii died at the wall? If the Sharaami soldiers were to be believed, they were killing three or four to every one of their own that fell. Gods, were there another few hundred thousand dead even now clawing their way up the city's walls?

Get up. Run. Stupid.

Peeling squirming intestines, slick with blood, from his limbs, he struggled to his feet. He didn't run. Couldn't. Half a million dead, in and around the city. The Tsarii could pack up and fuck off. Sharaam was doomed.

The dead clung to one another for support, aided each other in gaining their feet. Those in the dark, those shadowed from the cancerous light in the sky, remained dead and motionless.

Someone screamed on the far side of the mob of corpses and half of them turned in reaction. More screaming. Horror. Waking to find the dead husband you tossed into the alley looming over your bed.

They don't have to come over the wall now. All they have to do is keep us trapped inside.

A man, his chest a gaping wound of shattered ribs and shredded flesh, reached for Tash. Swollen fingers, pale sausages near bursting, fumbled at him.

You don't spend years practicing stabbing people, and occasionally stabbing people, without developing some muscle memory. Tash's arm flashed out and buried a knife in the dead man's eye socket.

The corpse winked at him. Or maybe it just blinked in surprise. So hard to tell with only one fucking curdled-milk eyeball.

Another knife out, spun in nimble fingers, and buried in the corpse's heart.

The dead man never broke eye contact.

Ha. Eye. Shouldn't it normally be 'eyes contact'?

Tash stabbed it three more times in various places that were either deadly, crippling, or sure to cause great agony, before that lizard core of fuck-everything-I-want-to-live at the base of his brain woke up and screamed, *Runyoustupidfucker!*

Fat fingers, vile green blood vessels visible through translucent flesh, gripped at Tash's shirt. Knocking the hand away, he swept the legs out from under the man, shoving him into the oncoming dead, and ran. Lurching corpses gave chase, stumbled into his path. He ducked past them, spinning and twisting. A corpse, half-buried in the filth, caught one of his boots, sending Tash sprawling to the ground.

Head ringing, he glanced down to see a dead girl of no more than twelve clawing her way up his leg. Whatever killed her had melted flesh, left her skull a bald and puckered wound. He kicked her in the face, shattering her nose. She didn't let go. Again and again, he kicked her, snapping her head to one side, tearing long strips of melted flesh with the sole of his boot, and still she refused to let go.

She said the word and he vomited. Luckily, most of whatever had once been in his belly already littered the ground elsewhere, so he only drooled bile down his chin and gibbered.

Fucking run!

Screaming terror and incoherent rage, Tash slashed the laces of his boot with the knife he'd forgotten was still clutched in his fist. Scrambling to his feet, he left the girl clutching her treasure as he sprinted awkwardly away.

The dead weren't fast, but they were damned strong.

Dodging around another knot of shambling corpses, Tash rediscovered a lesson he'd learned long ago as a child: the streets of Sharaam are no place for bare feet. He ran through the remains of a shattered whiskey bottle, vicious curved shards impaling the soft sole of his left foot. Dead filled the street, pouring out from every alleyway. He couldn't stop. They'd get him for sure.

Whimpering, he limped away.

Exiting the alley into a large town square, he saw clumps of living people fighting the corpses, battering them with clubs and chair legs, or hacking at them with swords and axes. Dismemberment seemed to be the only thing that stopped them. Hack the head off, and the body flailed blindly, still trying to kill you.

The wretched new sun spat and cracked above, a foul god glaring hate.

Across the square, he saw a storefront he recognized, and realized he knew the area.

He needed somewhere to hide. Somewhere to get away from this.

He limped faster. That sparking spitting green light overhead twisted his stomach.

Got to get out. Got to find Pitt.

The shard of glass in his foot found a nerve and he collapsed to the street with a squeal of agony. Fingers filthy and wet, he couldn't get a good enough grip on the blood-slicked glass to pull it free.

Worms in blood.

Casey bleeding out on the floor of The Dripping Bucket.

Tash crawled away, dragged himself into a sheltered doorway. There was a corpse there and he screamed again, but it was dead, motionless. An elderly woman, fat and swelling with bloat, taking up too much valuable space.

My hiding spot.

He shoved it out into the street so he could burrow further into the shadow. Nothing mattered more than escaping that terrible light.

The moment the fat old lady was lit green from above, she twitched and then said that unhearable word, wrenching another stomach-churning bout of nausea from Tash. He watched, drooling bile down the front of his shirt, as she pushed to her feet and staggered away.

The light.

Tash remembered the dead in the alley, how the ones sheltered in shadow didn't move, didn't rise with the others. The old woman in this doorway had been dead—proper dead—until he pushed her into the street.

Somehow that cancerous fire in the sky was bringing the dead to life.

Not life, Tash corrected.

Even though they moved with purpose, said that one awful word, those things weren't alive.

A Tsarii horn sounded far to the east, from beyond the wall. The dead stopped fighting, stood, heads tilted as if listening. Some of the Sharaami used the distraction to chop down their enemies. Most used it to flee. Again, the horn, a long peeling note, and the dead turned as one and headed east.

Tash watched.

The city wall.

But he had other concerns.

Worms in blood.

That thing in The Bucket hadn't chased him because it knew he was dead. Nothing else made sense. Somehow, he was infected. He imagined pinworms twisting through his veins, infesting his organs, making their way to his heart.

Cowering in the doorway, he dragged his wounded foot up and squinted at it. A hint of wrinkled fish-belly-pale skin in shadow.

Gods knew what damage he'd do if he kept running around with broken glass in his foot. And it slowed him. He needed to be faster!

Drawing one of the many knives hidden about his person, Tash touched it to flesh.

Cold. So cold.

What would he do if he discovered the worst? What if he found worms?

Get a medicker. Find a sorcerer. Someone somewhere had to be able to undo whatever had been done to him. Simonsi, he thought, lips like pillows, offering her alchemical cures. And he'd show her his bare wounded foot and tell her a bag-lady demon with meat-rot breath was so pissed with him she might have put worms in his bloodstream...

"Hey, Si, babe. You remember when we were first dating, and you had to mix that ointment? For the ... Yeah, the smell. Well, it's kind of, like that, only..." Ignorance might not be bliss, but it seemed a fuck of a lot better than your hot ex knowing some things.

Gritting his teeth, he dug out a large shard of jagged glass, moaning and whimpering. Cold steel felt like fire.

Blood trickled down his shin and dripped hot from his toes. Huddled in the shadows it looked black.

Too dark. Can't see the worms.

He started to stick his foot into the green light to better see. And stopped.

That thing in the sky brought back the dead. What would it do to exposed blood? Could it get him through an open wound? But then if he didn't expose that foot, he couldn't see if he was infected.

Fuck!

He couldn't decide which was scarier: being turned into a shambling zombie or learning that he was soon going to die from wormy blood.

Fucking moot, isn't it?

Sheathing the knife, he searched the cut, questing for the wriggling of small, squirming life. Blood slicked everything. Would he be able to feel them? Had that been real?

This is useless!

Unwilling to stick his foot into the light so he could see, and unable to feel anything in the blood, Tash tore a strip off his tattered, filthy shirt and wrapped it around his foot in a quick and sloppy tourniquet. Returning his attention to the street, he found it empty, the dead having disappeared to the east.

They're going to attack the wall from within.

He remembered the roar of the Tsarii as they attacked the wall when the new sun was born. The Sharaami defenders would be fighting the Tsarii when the dead ambushed them from behind. The corpses moved pretty slowly. If he ran, he might make it to the wall to warn the soldiers. He could save the city.

The gash on his foot throbbed.

How many dead were heading for the wall? All of them? Were there a hundred thousand corpses, or more, between him and the city's defenders?

And you want to run over there on your wounded foot and play the hero?

"Fuck that sideways with a shit-covered pitchfork," Tash told the empty street. Bravo. Tough guy. Swears a lot. Some other fool could save the day, Tash needed to focus on saving his own arse first. The loud swearing made him feel like he was justified in that. Not running the other way because he was shit scared or anything. Running the other way because he was the kind of cool guy who didn't give a toss.

He was left with the very lonely, very sad question: How am I going to save my own arse?

There was, he realized, only one very lonely, very sad answer: Pitt.

Pitt offered escape from the siege as payment for killing the king. No way the man didn't have a way out of the doomed city. Normally The Dripping Bucket was the first place Tash would look for the bastard, but no fucking way he was going back there. Luckily, there were other taverns, other hangouts for the city's cutthroats, murderers, and assassins.

Pitt would be in one of them.

Tash, feeling better about having a plan, glanced up and down the street. Still no sign of that girl, demon thing, whatever the fuck it was. That had to be good. He'd lost it.

Yeah? How'd it find you at the Bucket?

That, he decided, was a very good question.

Or maybe it wasn't. The Bucket was the first place he would have looked for Pitt, had he not already agreed to meet him there. Hell, the Bucket was the first place everyone looked when they wanted to hire someone dangerous. And maybe there was a leak somewhere on Pitt's side, someone spilling secrets to the King or the damned Tsarii or whomever. Yeah, that made more sense than some weird little pudding of a girl somehow following Tash—one of Sharaam's best assassins, maybe even the best now that Qwneera and Geln were dead.

He headed for the Rianican Church, an old monastery converted into a brothel and tavern down near the docks. The Church was known for a rotgut whiskey commonly referred to as bog water by the locals. Many a morning Tash had spent in the shite-house moaning in agony, crapping out his guts and swearing he'd never drink again. The Church was also a great place to get stabbed or find someone to do some stabbing. Back before he made his name, Tash spent three years there picking up odd gigs, mostly killing unfaithful husbands and occasionally bedding the now-widowed wives. Weird how killing their husbands made some women horny.

Collins ran the Church and had done so for two decades. To this day, Tash still lived by the old man's personal code: never pass up a chance to rut, piss, eat, or drink free beer. Surrounded by whores and ale, sufficeth to say Collins looked years older than the sixty he claimed. Scarred and pocked as he might be though, the old man always had a wench on his arm and a free pint for Tash.

Overhead, that sputtering cancerous ball of fire seemed to follow him.

* * *

THE CHURCH LOOMED large and dark, a monument to a long-dead and forgotten religion. Tash couldn't remember what the Rianican Sisters had worshipped. Some monster goddess of fingers and tongues and long, shuddering orgasms, or something. Centuries gone, nothing remained of them.

A dozen lanterns lit the Church in wavering yellow light, the smoke staining the forty-foot ceiling in clouds of blue.

"Tash," bellowed Collins, seeing the young assassin. "You look fucking terrible!"

Tash bellied up to the bar across from the owner. "Rough day. A mug of the bog, if you'd be so kind."

"I see you lost a boot," said Collins, grabbing a tin mug and giving it a perfunctory wipe with a questionable rag.

"Nonsense. I know exactly where it is."

Collins raised a bushy eyebrow in question.

"In the hands of the girl who attacked me."

"Women always did seem to like you."

"Did I mention she was dead?"

"That explains the stench. I thought maybe you'd been rolling in corpses."

Glancing down, Tash realized he was soaked through with gore. "Not far off." He tried wiping himself, but his hands were even worse. "Pour me a drink and I'll tell you a tale of necromancy and bravery."

Collins issued a soft grunt of amusement. "Bravery." He poured a measure into the dented cup and placed it on the bar.

Sipping and wincing at the flame the drink lit in his gut, Tash launched into a much-embellished version of his run-in with the dead. He told how he fought off a dozen of them, dismembering ravening corpses, and how he saved the children from that orphanage to the south—no, not the one that had been hit by Tsarii alchemicals, obviously a different one—and how grateful the nuns were.

Collins nodded along, refilling the mug as needed. "There were too many to fight through to get word to the boys on the wall that they were about to be attacked from behind?" he asked.

Tash shook his head in grim regret. "Tens of thousands. Even I couldn't have fought my way through so many. Plus, I had to see the children to safety."

"Right. The children."

"And I hurt my foot. Slowed me down."

"The foot," agreed Collins.

"Say," said Tash. "Do you know Pitt?"

"Ugly fucker? Retired soldier? Mean in a fight?"

"Yeah," said Tash, though he knew next to nothing of the man who'd hired him to kill the king.

"He drinks here sometimes with what's left of his squad."

"Squad?" He hadn't realized Pitt didn't work alone. "They were grunts? Why weren't they called to the wall? Fucking cowards."

"Grunts?" Collins shook his head, pouring himself a mug and finishing it in a single swallow. "Nah. They were a hit team. Assassinations. Infiltration. You don't waste a Shroud on grunts."

Shroud? Fucking hell!

Why had they hired Tash to kill the king? They could have done a much better job.

"The Shroud drinks here?"

"Hell no. Sometimes she *appears* here. She walks through the walls and says something weird to Pitt. But mostly she stays outside. Pitt once told me she didn't like it here because of all the dead gods begging her to let them outa the third basement."

"I didn't know you had a second basement."

"Apparently. I went looking and found stairs behind a crumbling bricked up wall. Had the wall rebuilt and doubled in thickness. Don't want no dead gods sneaking up and demanding free drinks!"

Marlene, one of Collins' whores, sidled up to Tash. Petite and fine boned, she looked like a porcelain doll with tits. "How do you do it?" she purred. "Covered in filth, stinking like a grave, but you're still cute." She picked something out of his hair, tossed it aside. "Maybe I can take you upstairs and get you a hot bath?"

"You have hot water?" Tash asked, darting a glance at Collins.

The old man rolled his eyes. "You should know better than to believe whores. Marlene, Tash is looking for Pitt. You seen him?"

"Nope. But Feylash is here. She's drinking alone. Been doing that a lot recently."

"How many she had?" Collins asked.

Marlene shrugged an exposed shoulder of pale flesh. "Six? Seven?"

"Stay away from her," the old man warned Tash. "In that state she'll either fuck you or kill you and both are the kind of trouble best avoided."

Tash glanced about the Church, but many tables had only a single patron slumped at them. No way to tell which one was this Feylash. "Really? Is she ugly?"

"The worst kind of ugly."

What the hells does that even mean? Is one ugly better than another?

As someone with chiselled features and the kind of eyes women swooned over, Tash couldn't decide. "Uh... open sores? Missing teeth?"

"Deeper."

Deeper? Tash shrugged off the question. It didn't matter what she looked like.

"She was the squad's Knife," said Collins as if that was supposed to mean something.

"And I'm an assassin." He resisted the urge to brag that he was now the best assassin in Sharaam. Collins hated braggarts.

Marlene pointed out a woman further along the bar. "That's her."

Grunting his thanks, Tash collected his mug and headed over. From behind, Feylash looked like so many women. Slim shoulders, back hunched as if expecting some dingus of a man to approach and try to talk her into bed.

He made it halfway to the woman before she rose and turned to face him. Startling green eyes. Hair red like the deepest flame. A narrow nose that stopped just shy of being pinched. She wore a vest of hardened leather, but even that hinted at interesting curves beneath. And there was nothing wrong with those legs! In truth, she was anything but ugly. Short, perhaps, certainly shy of five feet tall, but hardly horrid. What the hells had Collins been on about?

Perhaps surviving his encounter with the dead had left him a tad horny. Hells, it had been some time since he'd been with anyone. *Can't a man hope for even two minutes of soulless not particularly enjoyable humping before the world ends?*

Tash held his hands out, showing empty palms. "Just want to talk.

I'm looking for Pitt."

Though he towered over her, she showed no fear. She studied him, green eyes roving over his broad chest and muscled shoulders, lingering on his bootless foot.

She wants me.

"And you are?" she asked, full lips forming words in such an interesting way.

"Tash."

"Ah. The third best assassin," she said, kicking out a chair for him and dropping back into her own.

"Actually," said Tash, slumping casually into the chair across from her. "I'm the best."

"Oh?" She raised a sharply hooked eyebrow, a thin white scar bisecting it at the peak.

"King Inishiil is dead," he said, lowering his voice. "I've come to collect payment."

She blinked at him. "Have a drink," she said.

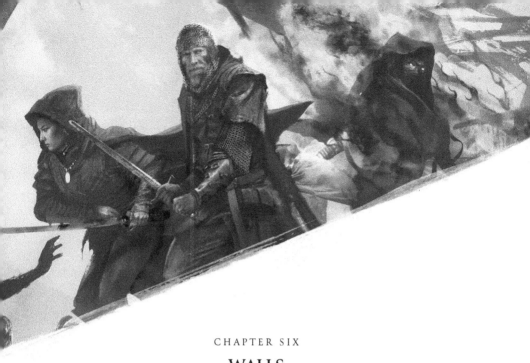

CHAPTER SIX

WALLS

A SCREAM RANG OUT, so loud the city seemed to break into pieces.

Lashiahar slumped against the stone wall of an alley, gasping. *Have we run far enough? Have we got away? The inn… the woman…* She thought: that was not a woman. She could remember Gertri's body collapsing, Pitt's shriek of grief, her own horror. No one should die like that, killed by something like that. Then the… the *demon*'s attention shifted for a moment. She had seized the chance, grabbed Pitt's arm, pulled him away screaming, and they fled.

I could just have run off alone, she thought, *as soon as the stupid lying useless failure fuck-up went in there. I have no idea why I didn't. Useless shit lied to me. But even in a warzone, even the enemy ... that woman, demon, her mouth opening like a void, and Gertri ...*

Lashiahar thought, hand touching her sword hilt: I refuse to let anyone die like that.

A fireball hung in the sky, sputtered and sparked, dripped bile on the city below. She felt more fear than she had ever known.

They had run for a long time, Lashiahar the Tsarii spy, Pitt, sometimes there was a third figure with them that was the thing, the *Shroud*, Wint. Lashiahar tried very hard not to look at Wint. No idea where they were going. Just ran until they couldn't breathe.

Then they had heard the scream.

Beyond the alleyway, torchlight flickered, there were voices shouting and calling, trumpets, the crash of metal. Lashiahar realized that she had led them almost into the shadow of the city walls. Trying to get back to her own people, she thought. Safety. Or, more likely, die with a few familiar faces around her, not alone in an enemy city she was sworn to destroy. For the last three years, she thought, I have worked day and night for this. And this useless fucker failed me. Fucking hopeless.

She *could* think: *and I hired the fucking hopeless useless fucker, so what does that make me except even more hopeless?* But she obviously wasn't going to think that. Nothing to do with me. All. His. Fault. Gov.

Even as they had fled, the sky had turned green and yellow, a vast ball of fire rising like a second sun. More Tsarii alchemicals. Nothing to be afraid of. Comforting, in fact: something that belonged to her side of the battle. She could imagine the munitions boys shouting at another successful launch, her old comrades nodding in satisfaction. Pitt, wheezing away as he ran, had barely bothered to look up. What is there to fear from alchemicals, when you've just seen a demon rip a woman to shreds? And they'd run on a few paces, Lashiahar half-listening out for the explosion when the munition hit. But the munition hadn't hit. The Shroud—Shrouds are real, demons are real, the stories they tell of this putrid city are all true, and a part of her thought, *oh, sweet Lord Thaliates, that's it, I can't take any more of this. They can court martial me for abandoning my post if they want to, but I give up, I'm fucking done here*—the Shroud had appeared almost solid beside Pitt, looked at the sky, and Lashiahar had had the sudden terrible impression that it—she—was frightened. To clarify: the thing that the demon had seemed scared of seemed to be scared of something. Lashiahar and Pitt had swung round in panic, thinking the demon must be there behind them at the least.

"It's… it's hunting us," Pitt said, the only thing he'd said since they fled from The Dripping Bucket. "Did you see the way it went for Gert? That's why none of the assassins could kill King Inshiil. He's got a demon guarding him."

And then, like a cheap bloody play-effect, the scream, and a flash of green light from the alchemical. And Lashiahar realized at the same moment as Pitt that it was the alchemical the Shroud was frightened of. It didn't fall. It didn't explode. It sat there, high in the arc of the bile-yellow sky, blazing down. It reminded Lashiahar of the demon's mouth biting down on Gertri.

"What's it doing?" Pitt asked. "Why doesn't it… explode or something?"

"It—" Another scream rang out. Might even be a human screaming.

Oh, sweet Lord Thaliates indeed. She realized then.

What it was.

"Rotting," the Shroud said, looking at the sky. "Death and life are rising."

"They did it." She didn't mean to say the words aloud. "They used it."

Pitt tried to tear his eyes away from the new sun. "Used what? Did what?"

All the time she'd been working her way through the city's underground, making contacts, her mission so heavy it crushed her, "We need someone to kill King Inshiil. Once he's dead, the city will surrender like that [snaps fingers]. You're the best, Lashiahar [big smile]. We're all relying on you." All the time, all the damned time, they'd been planning this.

She said dumbly, "I didn't know. No one... no one thought they'd actually do it."

"Do what, Tsarii?" Pitt screamed.

A boy without anything below his waist appeared around the corner of the alley. He was going very fast on his arms, leaving a smear of blood and... stuff behind him. He crawled over a lump of masonry and his intestines spooled over it, glistening. Like a thread had coming loose on a hem. Bits of half-digested food coming out the end.

Pitt hacked at the boy's body, smashed at it with his sword, kicked at it. Even as he cut it up, took its arms off, took its head off, it grabbed at him, tried to claw and bite him. Intestines wriggled like worms. Bits of the boy's body, minced meat, hacked up chunks, oozing back towards Pitt. The Shroud stood motionless. Finally, the thing was in bits so small it was no longer really moving. Just sort of... wobbling. Pitt bent over and was sick. Lashiahar had to fight hard not to join him. From beyond the alleyway a voice rose in a howl, abruptly cut off. The alchemical sun was a rancid wound.

"The light is a... a spell. To raise the dead," Lashiahar said.

Silence. Pitt looked at her. Looked at the mush at his feet. Dead meat and broken bone fragments oozed, still trying to kill him.

"Is that... tomato skin? Where did this kid get tomatoes? I haven't had a tomato in months..." He shook himself. His face was like a little child's. Baby's eyes, begging. "No one can raise the bloody dead."

A noise behind them, scrabbling. A dog leaped at them, snarling, on three broken slumps of legs. Half its head was missing. Both its eyes. Maggots in its eye sockets, churning.

The Shroud was a blur of movement, soft white robes, a gentle musk scent. The dog crumpled, cut to pieces. Dust and dry bone. It must have been dead for weeks. Even the maggots in its eyes looked dead.

Pitt whispered, "What the fuck have you people done?"

They began to go forwards again. After a few steps Pitt whimpered, staring down: Lashiahar kicked and stabbed… something bloody out of their way, took brief intense satisfaction in treading down hard on what might have been… another bit of… bloody thing. The alleyway opened into a little square with a fountain, a tree dying in the corner, a tavern with a bright painted sign. It must once have been a pleasant place to stop for a drink. A soldier's body writhed beneath a great lump of marble, pinned down and crushed beneath the statue that had once crowned the fountain. Pitt stopped, stared down. Green-tinged rotting hands and a black rotting face raised themselves frantically at him.

"It's trapped. It can't hurt you," Lashiahar managed to say. Pitt crept closer. Bent towards it. His own body shook. "Pitt!" It lashed a skeletal hand in his face. Pitt leaped back. Shrieked. His sword came down and down and down on the rotten body. Meat and bones and the last traces of a human face crumbled away to filth.

Pitt whispered, "Why? How could anyone do this?"

You're the head of a gang of vicious amoral hired killers. You tell me. I'm just a dedicated Tsarii patriot.

I'm sorry. I'm so, so sorry, Pitt.

"We wouldn't have needed to do it," Lashiahar said, "if you'd managed to kill King Inshiil." The Shroud hissed, as if naming him might summon his demon guardian. A flicker of fear cut through Lashiahar. What if it could?

Demons are real. Shrouds are real. This city is cursed, she thought. Why do we even want to take it? A dead crow, fat as a Thaliatesday turkey, flapped past overhead. A live crow, possibly even fatter, flapped after it trying to peck at it. Carrion, innit? A third crow, could have been dead or alive, mangy fucker, flapped after the second crow trying to peck at… there's a metaphor in there somewhere. I think.

I'm so sorry, Pitt. Honestly, I swear, I didn't know.

"The Shield," the Shroud said. In the ruined square, in the ruins of the soldier's body, in the ruins of Lashiahar's hopes for anything beyond dying here in failure… the Shroud's voice was so beautiful it made her heart ache. "Dying. Dead. Too difficult."

"We didn't know about the bloody demon."

The Shroud said, "All is lies. The Shield is dead."

The woman's thin mouth, fat dumpty grey body, fat little hands… No one should die like that. Lashiahar said, "I have some honour. I'd never have sent you, if I'd known about the demon." She met Pitt's dead-eyed hateful gaze straight-on: "Look, I mean… what would have been the point?"

Fragments of dry broken bone were still rattling across the flag-stones around them. Still trying to move, fight, alchemical magic shivering through them. And a growing rumble of noise from the direction of the walls. Lashiahar turned her head, tried to work out what was happening. A silver glow in the air? Shouting. And… a crash. From the walls, she thought. The walls! She realized suddenly that the alchemical bombardment into the city had stopped.

She said, "It should… The light will fade soon. The spell should… wear off."

"The dead will die again?" the Shroud said in her beautiful voice.

"The spell is only temporary," Lashiahar said. "Of course it's only temporary. Just… brief… To frighten people. Then the dead are… dead again…"

* * *

TEMPORARY, THOUGHT PITT. *The spell will end.*

That was good.

Good?

Nothing was fucking good. There was eyeball-deep in syphilitic arse-vomit and the other option, if you were really fucking lucky, was nostrils-deep in the same.

"I don't feel lucky," Pitt muttered to himself.

"What?" demanded Lashiahar.

"Eyebrows and sinking," said Wint, as if she heard his thoughts. She faded, became translucent and white, ghostly flickering like she was about to depart this reality forever. "Gertri knows," she whispered. "And she knows. Devours. Is. Us. The where the when. Following." The Shroud barked a frighteningly human laugh and once again solidified, became real. "My only."

"Your only what?" asked Pitt.

Had the Shroud seen something? Did she know something? Have something?

"Ships bad," said Wint. "The death beneath. But not there. Gone. Returned."

"Great," said Pitt.

The Shroud had always hated ships, hid in the hold among the rats every time work sent them somewhere distant. But the harbour was across town, and it didn't matter because the blockading Tsarii warships sank everything that left dock.

Overhead, that terrible new sun spat and sparked.

Temporary, Pitt decided, was too fucking vague. He turned on Lashiahar, didn't at all like the terror he saw there. "How long is temporary?"

"Rumour was that two Necrot travelled with the army. One carries the Stone of the Second Sun." The spy glanced up at the bilious light, winced. "She can maintain the spell as long as she remains awake. As long as her sanity holds. The other is to take it when she falters."

Lashiahar shrugged. "The reports I read on testing the spell said it ate most Necrots in a matter of hours. Sometimes less."

Hours. With two of them, maybe half a day. Not great, but better than weeks or months.

The wall only has to hold for hours.

The Tsarii had been throwing themselves at the wall for weeks. What were a few more hours?

There weren't dead before.

Or rather, there were, but they were dead dead. Proper dead, so to speak.

"These Necrot can control the dead they've raised?" he asked.

Lashiahar hesitated and did something that was a cross between a shrug and a nod.

Fucking great.

Eyebrows and sinking, indeed.

"I need to see," decided Pitt.

Can't make decisions without the information.

It made sense, but at the same time he knew he was stalling. What would he see from the wall that might change things? Would there be a sudden revelation, '*Oh, look, a postern gate no one on either side has ever noticed before, there's our way out!*'? No. No there fucking wouldn't be.

Curiosity was a motherfucker.

They were very near the city walls now. Pitt pointed ahead. Ramparts swarmed with Sharaami soldiers. A fortified set of stone steps led to the top. It swarmed with troops heading to the wall, and messengers descending with their reports.

"Follow," he ordered, setting off.

Surprisingly, they did. He had no idea why. Wint was constantly disappearing through walls. She could probably wander out of this city any time she wanted. Why she hadn't already was a mystery he wasn't too interested in examining. What was it Anukat always said?

Oh yeah, don't look a gift camel in the arse.

Lashiahar was an enemy spy and his crew had failed to do the job she'd hired them for. Why was she still with him? Why hadn't he killed her already and been done?

All gonna die anyway.

Not much point in killing her.

And maybe she'd be useful.

Pitt shoved his way through soldiers, falling back into old patterns. He barked orders, screamed abuse, and generally acted as if he outranked even the gods. Pretend you're in charge, and soldiers are generally happy to let you be. Weird that this never really worked with Gertri. Not a day passed when he didn't feel like she was letting him pretend to be in charge and the moment he fucked up or made a really dumb decision she'd knife him and take over the squad.

Thinking of her hurt. Stabbed pain into his chest.

Oh, Gertri, I'm sorry.

He wasn't sure why. All he asked her to do was wait in a fucking tavern and maybe kill that half-wit, Tash! How dangerous should that have been?

Partway up the steps a hulking bear of a sergeant got in Pitt's face, demanding to see his orders. Pit screamed incomprehensible rage and spittle. The sergeant refused to budge.

Wint ghosted forward, passing so close to Pitt his entire right side went numb. The sergeant made a choked sobbing noise and curled up on the steps, crying. He smelled like he shit. Stepping over him, Pitt stopped.

All along the wall, scaling ladders rose. Thousands of them.

Screaming. Chaos.

"For Sharaam! Hold the wall you goat-fucking cowards!"

The Tsarii wailed back in their incomprehensible gibbering. Didn't sound like war-cries to Pitt, but who could tell?

Sharaami soldiers dumped boiling oil on the scalers. Threw rocks. Stabbed faces and cut off hands as they reached the top.

A young Tsarii, all acne and wispy moustache and greasy hair, made it onto the wall. Instead of fighting to clear a space for those following, he shoved into the press of Sharaami soldiers, heading for the steps Pitt stood on. Someone stuck a sword in the kid's throat and the Tsarii went down, gagging. There were more of them. Not one of the Tsarii was interested in a fight. They didn't attack. The Sharaami weren't enemies, they were obstructions. The enemy shoved them back, drove them back down the steps with sheer force of numbers. Shoved back, Pitt retreated before the press.

More and more poured over the wall.

"They aren't fighting," he screamed at Lashiahar. "Why aren't they fighting?"

A Tsarii staggered off the ladder he'd ascended. Seeing the mad swarm of chaos on the wall, he tried to jump down into the city instead of taking the steps. A forty-foot plummet: he landed badly, shattering his skull. Then, skull a misshapen half-crushed melon, he rose and started killing. The Tsarii youth with the acne stood, throat a gaping wound, and bit someone's face off. Just fucking scraped it off with his teeth like he was eating corn on the cob.

"Time to go," said Pitt.

Turning, he fled back down the steps.

Wint and the spy followed, the Shroud floating.

Apparently, everyone—Sharaami and Tsarii alike—had the same idea.

Soldiers of both sides streamed past Pitt, sprinting into the city, fleeing whatever chased them up the wall.

Soldiers who had stood against the invaders for weeks, fought bravely in spite of the sure knowledge they could not win, broke and ran.

Off the stairs and into the streets.

Letting the weight of numbers decide his direction, Pitt struggled to form a plan. Where should they go?

Warriors swarmed by, running in every direction. A Sharaami archer tripped and fell and two Tsarii picked him up and ran with him until he got his feet under him again. The three ran on. Holding hands.

The fuck?

Enemies no longer enemies.

That could only mean one thing.

There was a scarier enemy.

Behind the Tsarii came the dead. They swarmed up the scaling ladders, poured over the walls like a hive of enraged ants. Thousands. Hundreds of thousands. Every Tsarii who'd died beyond the wall. Every corpse the Sharaami defenders had dropped over the wall towards the Tsarii camp. The dead didn't care about steps. They fell the forty feet and then lay there flailing, bones shattered and jutting from torn flesh. Those coming after landed on a carpet of writhing corpses and were undamaged enough they could stand and give chase to the living.

Any semblance of this being a war—of there being an us versus them—degraded to madness. The dead fought without intelligence, battled without a plan. There were so many of them, it didn't matter. They surrounded the living and cut them and turned them into yet more murderous dead. Dead Sharaami fought alongside dead Tsarii invaders.

Pitt ran and the others followed. If they hadn't, he wouldn't have slowed.

"Ha," he said, wheezing.

"What?" shrieked Lashiahar, running at his side.

A score of corpses that must have come over the wall somewhere else got in front of them and Wint turned them into red pudding. Pitt splashed through the ruin and kept running.

Where?

Someone said something about the docks.

Yeah! The docks! With the Tsarii as interested in getting out as the locals, maybe the blockade had lifted.

"Fucking what?!" Lashiahar shrieked.

"You didn't win the war!" Pitt crowed, cackling.

She laughed, coughed, and laughed again as she ran at his side. "Only a fucking Sharaami would call this winning."

CHAPTER SEVEN

AT THE DOCKS

EYLASH WAS SHORT and funny and sexy and got shorter, funnier, and sexier the more drinks Tash banged back.

Maybe the shorter part was a lie.

The more he drank, the more interesting she became, and the less interested in him she appeared to be. At first, she was very curious, indeed. How had he killed the king? How had he escaped? How was he going to spend his pay once they got out of Sharaam? He wove a tale of bravery and heroism, working in a cast of background characters. He told her about how he rescued the kids at the orphanage, fighting off hordes of corpses, but the more he talked the more interested she became in the door.

Collins had dug up a single boot to replace Tash's missing one. It didn't fit and smelled like someone had been using it as a lavatory for decades, but beggars couldn't be… whatever the opposite of beggars was.

"What's the opposite of beggars?" he asked Feylash, looking up from her cleavage.

A man stood behind her chair, towered over her. He looked like someone crossed a gorilla, a bear, and an oak tree and then stuffed the result in leather and chain armour. A beard mobbed the face, claiming most of the available territory. It might have been red, or that might have all the blood. It leaked, unnoticed, down his neck. Ice shard blue eyes studied Tash, shocking above the gory beard and ridged tribal scars.

"Anukat," said Feylash without looking up. "If you drip blood on me, I swear to fuck I will beat you unconscious with your own cock."

The giant grinned and reached out a hand as if to fondly ruffle her hair.

"Don't," she said. Her gaze didn't leave Tash.

The man hesitated, eyes narrowed.

"I can hear you thinking," said Feylash.

The beast growled, showing bloody teeth, massive hands forming two meaty fists with the crunch of knuckles.

"Almost there," she said. "Come on. So close."

"That's the only thing," grunted the barbarian, "big enough to kill me."

"Gods that was painful."

Shrugging, the giant collapsed into a chair. "Where's Pitt?"

"This," she said, gesturing at Tash, "is the assassin we hired to kill the king. He has just reported his success."

Anukat dashed a confused look from Tash to Feylash. "And he came to you?"

The little redhead rolled green eyes with a sigh of wearied patience.

"Well," said Anukat. "I thought, you know, he wouldn't want to."

Feylash waited.

"You know," said the monstrous barbarian. "Because of what happened."

"What happened?" asked Feylash.

"Nothing."

"I swear to fuck I'm going to kill you."

Anukat grinned like this had been his goal all along. "Maybe it wasn't nothing," he admitted. "Nothing never really happens. Not really. There's always something."

Collins brought Anukat the biggest mug of ale Tash had ever seen and deposited it before the bear.

"It comes in buckets?" Tash asked.

Collins grunted. Arm shaking from the strain, he held a second equally huge mug in his other hand.

Anukat grinned thanks and drained it in a go. Collecting the empty mug, Collins dropped the other in its place and left.

"You were saying?" prompted Feylash.

Wiping a froth of foam from his mouth, Anukat said, "There's always something happening but sometimes it's not what you were hoping."

"I've had turds smarter than you," said Feylash. "Stop trying to be philosophical. It's bad enough when Pitt does it."

"Sometimes the thing that happened isn't what you paid to make happen."

"Ah," said Feylash.

"Ah," said Tash. "Shit."

Feylash gave Tash a lingering look that was a lot less friendly than the previous lingering looks. "You said you killed the king."

"A slight exaggeration," admitted Tash.

"Did you wound the king?" she asked.

"Very nearly."

"Were you ever in the same room?"

"Quite almost."

"A scullery maid chased him out of the castle about thirty seconds after he went in," said Anukat.

Tash held up his hands in protest. "She was a demon."

"We should kill him," said Feylash. "Kill him and then go find Pitt and Gert and that the damned spy."

Anukat nodded happily, leaning his chair back onto the rear two legs. "See? I didn't think he'd search us out, because now we have to kill him!"

You don't get to be the third best assassin in Sharaam by being slow or hesitating. Tash kicked the big barbarian's chair out from under him and spun a knife at the redhead's throat.

* * *

TASH WOKE LYING on the floor staring up at Pitt, Feylash, Anukat, and some pinch-faced woman he didn't recognize. They looked like they'd had a food-fight in an abattoir. Something faded in and out behind them, blurry and indistinct. Sometimes he thought it was the most beautiful woman. Sometimes it was bones and hollowed death and he thought maybe he'd cracked his skull open against the floor.

"Ow," he said.

The redhead spun his knife between her fingers in a smooth blur. She did it like other people picked their nails or chewed their lips: without conscious volition. The knife rolled across the back of her knuckles and spun in the other hand.

"He's not dead," said Pitt. "Why isn't he dead?"

"He made Anukat spill beer all over himself," said Feylash, "and that was the funniest thing I've seen in years."

The big tribal monstrosity, now soaked in ale and blood, nodded. "It was well done," he admitted.

Pitt scowled at Tash. "He's not dead because he spilled beer?"

Feylash and Anukat nodded. "Essentially," said the redhead. "That and he mentioned a demon."

The blurry thing snapped into focus and looked like a woman dressed in filthy dishrags. "Choosers. And the answer is going to be no," she hissed at Tash. "And yes, there is." She faded back to blurry.

"What?" Tash asked.

The pinch-faced woman said, "He wasn't lying about the demon. Unfortunately. But we have bigger problems."

Bigger than the demon? She was clearly deranged.

Even Pitt looked sceptical. "Lashiahar," he said, nodding to the pinch-faced woman, "meet Tash. I'd say he was the worst assassin money can buy, but he hasn't actually killed anyone. Tash," he added, "this is Lashiahar, the Tsarii spy who hired us to kill our king."

Lashiahar scowled at Tash. "I can't believe you hired an ugly cut-rate sewer rat—"

"Hey!" protested Tash. "If I cleaned up, I'd look—"

"—after I paid you three hundred gold!"

"—pretty good. Three hundred? Pitt, you cheap fucker you only offered—"

"You didn't kill him," Pitt roared at Tash, "so it doesn't fucking matter!"

"He has you there," said Anukat. "Not in a great bargaining position." He glanced at Feylash. "Timing's not great either."

The redhead didn't seem to notice. Lips pursed, she kept looking toward the door.

"Ale?" said Anukat.

"Yes," said Pitt, collapsing into a chair.

"Fuck yes," agreed the spy, sitting beside him.

The tribal bent down, grabbed Tash by the collar, hoisted him effortlessly into a chair, and then sat too. Only Feylash and the ghost woman remained standing.

"Fey," said Pitt. "What's wrong?"

With a flick of nimble fingers, Tash's knife disappeared. "I'm done," Feylash said.

"Hey," mumbled Tash, "I need that."

"We're heading to the docks," Pitt said, ignoring Tash. "We're getting out."

"No," said Feylash. "I like you lot. That's bad. Emotions are a weakness." She tousled Anukat's hair and then wiped her bloody palm on Pitt's armour, leaving a red smear among the other red smears. "Better on my own. Nothing to slow me down."

"We're better together," said Pitt, eyes pleading.

"Weakness only," said the ghost woman, shrouds floating about her as if underwater.

Tash's heart sank as Pitt got this haunted look, like the ugly bastard somehow knew what the ghost meant.

"Weakness only?" Pitt asked.

"Weakness only," agreed the ghost.

"Fuck that," said Tash, making to stand. "Some people might be a weakness, yeah, but some of us are a strength. I'm coming with you."

Feylash pushed him back into his chair. "You're cute, but dumber than a bag of drowned kittens."

"Weakness only," repeated the ghost.

"Fuck." The huge warrior nodded to the short woman. "It's been…"

"Terrible," finished Feylash.

Pitt looked like he desperately wanted to ask her to stay. Instead, he lifted his pint and said, "Raise one for me later."

"If I haven't forgotten your name by the time I reach the street," said Feylash.

Turning, she left the Church without another word.

Only Tash watched her leave. Everyone else focussed on their drinks.

I should follow her.

He didn't. Wasn't sure why.

"So," said Pitt.

"Any point?" asked Anukat.

Pitt shrugged. "You always try. That's..." He shrugged. "You just do."

"What just happened?" asked Tash. Now that it looked like he might not get murdered in the next few seconds, he wanted to get out of here. "What does 'Weakness only' mean?"

"Is she ever wrong?" asked Lashiahar.

"How the fuck would we know?" said Anukat.

Tash emptied his mug. "I just had a brilliant fucking idea." When all eyes were on him, he continued. "Collins told me that your ghost lady thingy—"

"Her name is Wint," said Anukat. "She's a Shroud."

"—said there were dead gods in the third basement," Tash finished. "And shrouds aren't real."

No one so much as blinked.

"Let them free. Let them fight the dead. Let them fight the Tsarii."

Hopeful eyes turned on the ghost woman.

"Wint already said no," said Anukat. "It was the first thing she said," he added when everyone turned on him. "'The answer is going to be no.' Don't you people listen?"

The ghost woman—Wint, the big tribal called her—became real long enough to say, "There are worse things than being dead," and faded before Tash could think of a quick-witted comeback.

"Well," he said, "there's nothing worse than being dead."

Anukat wrung blood and beer out of his beard, leaning forward so the result landed in his bucket-like mug. "The other thing Wint said is 'Yes, there is.' You really gotta pay more attention." He drank from the bucket.

"Seeing as we don't need this failed assassin," said the Tsarii spy, "shall we kill him and be on our way?"

"A failed assassin," said Tash, "is more useful than a failed Tsarii spy. In fact," he looked from Pitt to Lashiahar, "I'd say everyone at this table has failed in some way."

"Got you there," said Anukat.

"And do you really want to make more dead that you're going to have to fight?" added Tash.

"Another good point," agreed Anukat.

"More swords on our side are better than less," said Pitt, looking unhappy about the decision.

"So," said Tash, leaning forward on the table, "what's the plan? I see you've kept the spy. I'm guessing she's our way out?"

Pitt winced and looked away, gazing longingly at the door. "We're going to the docks."

"The Tsarii sink everything that leaves the harbour."

"The walls have fallen," said Pitt. "Sharaam is lost."

"The damned Tsarii won?"

The grizzled warrior grunted a laugh. "Hardly. That spell," he waved a hand towards the window and the weird greenish light pouring in, "didn't work as they expected. The dead overran the invaders, chased them into the city. The war is over. It's the dead against the living. At least until the spell stops." He glanced at Lashiahar. "Why hasn't it stopped?"

She gave a helpless shrug.

"Anyway," Pitt continued, "we're hoping the blockade will lift once they see all the Tsarii in the city."

"Hoping?" asked Tash. "Fuck. I was hoping you had an actual plan."

Rising from the table, Pitt ignored him. When the others stood too, Tash grunted and pushed to his feet. His head still hurt.

Somehow, Wint was already outside, staring up at the spitting sun. Aunkat headed out the door with Pitt close on his heels. The scarred old man held the door for Lashiahar like she was royalty, and then let it swing closed on Tash.

Useless fuck. Fawning over the fucking Tsarii spy.

I should abandon them, go it alone like Feylash.

Maybe he could still find her.

Out into the false day, all thought of being alone or going in search of the cute redhead died.

He hadn't been in the Rianican Church more than an hour or two, but he no longer recognized his city. Sharaam burned, a hellish glow in every direction except the docks. Smoke choked the air. Thick black ash fell like snow. The streets were crammed with wide-eyed faces, soot-stained and stinking of fear. Tsarii and Sharaami alike worked to build a barricade blocking the harbour from the rest of the city. They tore houses and wagons apart with their bare hands, throwing everything onto a growing mound of detritus.

"That won't last long," said Pitt. "They swarmed over the fucking wall like it was nothing. A pile of garbage won't slow them." Rimmed with exhaustion, horror haunted his eyes. "Once they've killed the rest of the city, made more dead, they'll come for the last of us."

Pitt said it like he thought the dead were planning, thinking beings. Having fought free of the things, Tash knew otherwise. Though the old fart was right about one thing: that pile of trash wouldn't stop them.

"Let's get to the docks," said Lashiahar. "I might be able to get us onto a ship."

Might? They didn't have a fucking ship already waiting?

Tash glanced toward the harbour. It was chaos down there, a mad crush of humanity fighting over the last boats. Hope was so slim it died of starvation.

Feylash was right. He'd be better off alone. These idiots were going to get him killed. Get out of the harbour district before the dead come. Find somewhere to hide.

Should he say something, suggest they hide together? No, that was stupid. They'd slow him down. Anukat was too damned big to hide, and Pitt too dumb. The spy… maybe she was hot, in an experienced older woman kind of a way, or would be if she wore a little less gore, but she was a spy. Only a fool asked for that kind of trouble.

Better not to say anything.

Best to slip quietly away.

Like the best fucking assassin in Sharaam.

Decision made, Tash lost himself in the crowd. The farther he got from Pitt, the better he felt. It was difficult to describe. Like, with them, he was a side character, the kind of expendable person who always died in some horrible way near the end of the story. Alone, however, he was the hero. What was the word the playwrights used? Pro tagonist? Did that make the background characters amateur tagonists?

No one this good-looking dies in the stories!

Kind of funny, really. You go to watch a play and as soon as you see the best-looking character, you know exactly who will survive.

Tash shook the thought off. Didn't fucking matter. Though someone should write a play about his life.

Time for a better plan than being stabbed in the back.

With all the city's survivors crammed into the harbour district, it was immediately obvious where the dead would come. And since the makeshift barricade wouldn't stop the dead, it was equally obvious this was the one place Tash didn't want to be. Really, now that he thought about it, the answer was obvious: be where everyone isn't.

He'd go over the barricade and into the city. Somewhere, he'd find a place to hide and stay there until all this blew over. Maybe a tavern, somewhere with food and drink.

Shoving through the crowd, most of whom were heading away from the hastily slung-together wall of crap, Tash reach the shit-heap. Tables and chairs, no doubt stolen from the nearest pub, had been thrown atop a line of overturned wagons. Armoires and broken coa-tracks. Blankets, towels, threadbare rugs. Bedframes and bookcases. Wooden toys and vacant-eyed dolls. If it could be dragged from a home or a business and tossed on the pile, it had been.

The few mad, deranged, or brave who'd decided to man this wall were uniformly filthy, stained cinereal with ash, eyes wide and terri-fied. They stank of fear.

Running a hand through his blond hair, brushing it back from his face, it came away black. When this was finished, he was going to have a long hot bath, and bed the first beautiful and willing woman he found. Maybe Simonsi, if she survived. Why had they broken up anyway? She was beautiful. He was beautiful. They were perfect together! And gods, those lips. Simonsi kissed like she put her soul into it.

Tash climbed the garbage wall, ignoring the yells and threats of the defenders. It was easy. Pitt was right: this wouldn't stop a child. Reaching the top, he came face to face with the first corpse climbing the other side. Reacting without thought, he chopped its legs out from under it, sending the thing tumbling back down.

Dead. As far as the eye could see. Lit yellowish green bile by the cancer sun, they mobbed the wall, clambering over it without so much as breaking pace. They hurled themselves at the defenders.

For a heartbeat, Tash stood unmolested. The dead filled every street beyond the harbourfront. Tsarii and Sharaami. Civilians and soldiers. Some ran. Some dragged themselves on shattered arms. Women and children. Severed limbs and organs hanging in looping coils that got caught on everything. Twitching lumps of meat.

The dead said that word and everyone manning the wall bent double, puking up their last meal. The ale Tash downed at the Rianican

Church returned, still cool and tasting much the same.

The world went from stinking of burnt flesh and wood and a few hundred thousand corpses to stinking of burnt flesh, wood, a few hundred thousand corpses, and vomit. Damned near qualified as an improvement.

When he finally managed to straighten, Tash gazed down upon the gathered dead. For a heartbeat, they stared back up at him. Like the world took a long breath, a pause in the shitstorm of reality.

Out among the corpses, a woman caught his eye. Stunningly gorgeous. Even dead. She wore a form-fitting black dress. Dark tattoos, arcane traceries, snaked her flesh. Long, black Tsarii hair tied in tight braids hung to her waist. And there, where the hair stopped, hung a cancerous greenish yellow globe. It sparked and spat.

Tash looked from the globe up to the false sun and back. They were identical. Both arced and spat at the same time, pulsing like the hearts of two entwined lovers.

Tsarii sorcerer. Whatever they were called. Necrot, or something.

Looking up from the curve of her hips, Tash met the woman's beautiful eye. The other was a ragged ruin, a knife buried to the hilt in the socket.

This is her spell.

He saw it all. The dead rising and flooding toward Sharaam, killing the Tsarii's enemies. But then she'd lost control and the dead turned on everyone. Someone, maybe one of her own soldiers or a general or something, thought that killing her might end the spell.

Bang. Dagger in the eyeball.

But the spell went on, and now she was dead and there was nothing to end it.

The globe hung there, so close. The Tsarii necrot couldn't have been more than a few rows into the mob. He could probably reach her before the dead brought him down.

And then what?

She was dead. What the ever-loving fuck could he do to her that a dagger in the brain didn't achieve?

Tash looked over his shoulder at the Harbour District. Ships burned. The ocean writhed and frothed with blood. The Tsarii fleet was flaming wreckage. Pitt was an idiot. There was no escape there. Even as he watched, the vast carcass of a long-dead whale humped itself half out of the water, the body of a newly dead fleeing soldier flapping in its teeth. A long-dead something with a beak and wings and tentacle reared up beside it in a broil of methane. And was that…? Gods, yes, a long-dead, very rotted mermaid. A lot of long-dead, very rotted flapping about like fish-out-of-water fish. Two men striking boldly out to sea on a makeshift raft yelled, started paddling back to shore, saw the dead surging towards them across the harbour, turned round again. The something's tentacles licked out. Dissolving into rancid jelly. Tash closed his eyes. When he opened them a moment later, the raft was gone. Long-dead poxing seagulls. Flash of long-dead shark's fins.

There was no salvation out there either. Tash focussed again on the woman and that globe of flickering cancer round her neck.

You're going to die here.

No. Not possible. He was too fucking cute to die. Nobody with cheekbones like his should die like this.

He had, he realized, two choices, neither of which were really choices. He could flee into the harbour and postpone his death. Or he could try and break that globe, pray that doing so ended the spell.

One ended in a terrible and ignominious death.

The other ended with a terrible and ignominious death and him saving all Sharaam and being the hero.

That's what the cheekbones are for, he thought.

Tash leapt off the wall of garbage and threw himself into the dead mob. Sword and knife lashing out, he spun and slid, ducking around reaching hands and gaping mouths.

Too fast. Can't catch me.

Chop off a groping hand.

Slide away from a coiling loop of intestine trying to trip him.

There she was.

Lifting his sword, Tash shouldered the last intervening corpse from his path.

The dead said their word and he was on his knees, retching bile from an empty stomach. He'd dropped his sword. Couldn't see it through the endless sea of legs. Dead everywhere. His throat closed with the abattoir stench. Kneeling in guts, hands wrist-deep in blood, he couldn't breathe.

Almost. So close.

Tash looked up, saw the woman, the globe hanging at her hip by a thin braid of golden rope.

The throwing knife. Countless thousands of hours spent practicing. Yes!

Reaching for the dagger, he found the scabbard empty.

Feylash. That trick where she made his knife disappear. *You're dumber than a bag of kittens,* she said.

Fuck.

Fuck fuck.

Cold dead hands gripped his ankle, entwined in his hair.

Tash lunged at the globe. Grabbing it, he tore it from the rope, the clasp coming apart.

He smashed the sickly thing against the street, shattering it and driving shards of glass into his fingers and palms.

The light died.

The cancerous false sun flickered and went out.

As one, the dead fell.

"I did it. I saved the city." Tash blinked at the shattered glass driven into his palms. "Holy fuck that hurts."

He was the hero. The best assassin in all Sharaam and the one man everyone would talk about after all this shit was cleaned up. There'd be parties and women and yet more women. Simonsi might even apologise for dumping him.

He pulled a sliver of glass from the base of his thumb. "Ow, fuck."

The king would hug him. He'd be knighted. Given lands and property. Yeah, no way Inishiil knew Tash had planned to assassinate him. A minor detail at best. Hardly worth a mention.

Kneeling among the dead, Tash looked up from his bloody hands.

There, not ten strides away, stood that frumpy girl. She'd been among the corpses. Why they'd ignored her, he had no idea. Somewhat worse for wear, her rough cotton shift was soaked in blood. Her hair hung in tangled, matted clumps, drooling blood down her face.

One greasy eye slid to focus on Tash.

"No," he whispered. "No, fuck no."

The other eye slid to join the first and he became the centre of her attention.

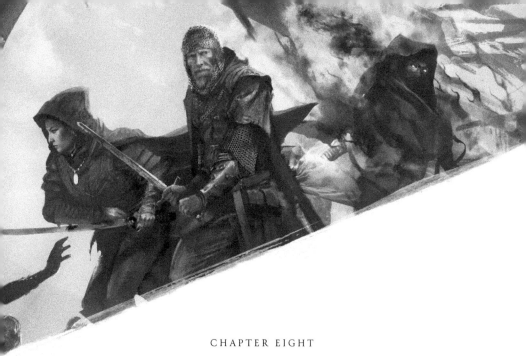

CHAPTER EIGHT

A BRIGHT BURST OF SUNLIGHT

I ANANR HAD MOVED through corpses as through deep water. Eternities, once, she had swum and drifted and sported herself in seas of writhing dying tendrilled limbs. The city her prison: blossoming. The sweetness! The perfume! This is how it was once, always, her past when the worlds were young when this was what she was. She trampled them beneath her body. Weak thin frailty of her human form, softness of her limbs, but these dead things, bloated already rotted, she can brush through them, choke herself and gorge herself on them. The pleasure of un-folding them before her, spiralling down into them as they unfurl themselves before her. Open. Like petals. Plunge deeper ever deeper, labyrinthine curls, the gleam, the colour trails, the scents and textures plunge deeper ever deeper swallow herself into them. These dead things.

And the sky! She saw, with human eyes and with her own eyes, the light of a sun that was beautiful. The sky was filled with wonder. The light was real. She could feel the warmth of it on her true skin. Iananr stood tall, raised her human arms.

In the new sun's light, she cast a shadow on the earth behind her.

She held out her hand, her real hand, moved it. A wave. Flicker of light and dark on the stones of a wall. Her hand's shadow: she made it dance. Elated, she turned, jumped, danced, kicked up her legs, threw her hair back. Two shadows on the wall behind her: her human shadow, fingers like branches tapping, hair like waves like cloudbursts as she danced; her true shadow, twisted, visible, turning and turning on the grey stone. A great burst of hope sprang up silvery inside her. In this new sun, she was brightened, warmed with happiness. What it was, she could not say. A gift, for her. When she had danced and watched her shadow dancing, she stood in the rubble of a house with the dead flowing in their streams around her, stood face raised to feel again the sunlight on her skin. How fine it was. How good. The weight of the chains was lessened, even. The goading, clenching voice, *Find it. Hunt it. Follow the trail. Go on.* The lash of the whip, the word-chains tighten. But to stand here, so briefly, warmed by the sun… She raised her human hand, held it up with the green light behind it, she could see her real hand black against the green light. The light green light was so bright now it hurt her eyes. Made her blink, throwing patterns behind her eyelids.

How long…? Days, moments, aeons, since she last felt the warmth of a sun.

Her face was bruised where the Shroud had hurt her. Wint. Cold woman's hands breaking through into her real body, damaged her.

Strange. A good feeling. Memory of real battles. What is it? How did it hurt me? Can it hurt me again? Really hurt?

I would like to be defeated, Iananr sometimes thinks. I have been here so long. Would my master let me be, release me, if I was defeated? If my master knew something here could harm me?

The word-chains tore at her. *Hunt! Find! Consume it! Destroy!* A thrill of pleasure, wet body memory, taste of iron, wriggling maggot-deep in the folds of her human skin. But the longing to stay here, move her human hands and her real hands, cast shadows with her real hands in the light of this new beautiful warm sun...

She thought: I am sated with killing. For a little while. I want—

Scent trail. Thick colour ooze of it. Distant. Distinct.

She watched with a flicker of recognition as the dead she had made crawled out from the ruins of the inn the Dripping Bucket, dragged themselves and threw themselves on the dead who still lived. Follow the trails. Find. Prey and hunter. This day of marvels! The new green sun on her face, and the thought, sudden, brilliant, that she had been hurt as she had not been hurt for eternities of weak lifetimes. Then the thought also, keener, hissing, that the being Tash had power such as she had not imagined.

Tash can... help me. Free me.

She began to run, awkward on the heaviness of her human legs. Thighs chafe against each other. Ripple of flesh and fat. The bones in her knees crack. Human lungs wheezing. Human spittle on dry human lips. A lock of her human hair, lank and greasy, getting into her eyes, catching with an itch on her lips and her cheek.

The scent trail curled ahead of her. Fear-taste and... joy-taste to it. She almost moaned in need.

Tash.

* * *

THE SCENTS OF the city were changing. New colours thick in the air that made her snort with disgust. Under the green light of the new sun, she began to notice that the soldiers stood together as allies. The army outside the walls, *accursed enemy filth*, the old master and King Inshiil called them, and the soldiers who tried to stop them getting in, *heroes. Our boys. Fucking shit useless pauper cunts but as long as they bloody hold the walls long enough*, the old master and King Inshiil called them. Different armour, she had begun to understand, let her tell them apart, if she looked closely enough. The same weight of death. But different armour, and sometimes their swords were different. The ones inside must have let the others come in.

Two of them still just living, back-to-back, almost knit together as one man, fighting five, six of them already dead.

"Help me!"

"Just fucking help me!"

"Sweet pale hells, thank fuck you're here with us!"

"This man is an enemy and I have spent many months fighting him, and I swore to kill him. But when his brother's corpse came at me, he saved my life."

"This man killed my brother with his own hands. But when my brother's corpse came at him today, I saved him."

"Brothers for life now, we are! And these dead together—we'll smite them!"

Two of them backed up against a wall, swords moving together, "This wasn't quite what I meant," the enemy filth said, "when I boasted I'd have your women gagging for me." They were overwhelmed, the pair of them, swallowed up in a wave of the dead. Wail of a man's voice muffled and crushed. A sword flailed, an arm reached upward, then lost. A scrabble of flesh, armoured hands erupted, the enemy filth cut his way up out of the corpses, dragged the hero cunt out beside him. They embraced, whooping. Ran off together hand in hand, two blood-soaked, filth-soaked swimmers in a bloody, filthy sea. "Kind of makes you think, doesn't it, when a real crisis hits… This whole, like, killing each other over who gets to collect our taxes thing suddenly seems, like, kind of a bit… pointless?"

"We'll build a better future, yeah, together, when this is over, right? Build back better? Everything can change?"

A figure lurched into her path. Iananr's hands went out to kill it. She saw at the last moment the grey face of the girl-child she had previously met. Her hands dropped, she stared at it. The girl stared back with eyes that were huge and shining and green-red. It smiled at her. Beneficent. Grateful. Iananr saw then that it had another child, a boy, a little younger, cowered behind it.

"My friend Mye," it said. The dead came shambling past, nails and teeth for killing, but the girl looked at them, smiled at them, and they ran away. The girl reached out its hands, so thin, so tiny, touched a dead man on the shoulder. Light—in the girl's eyes, in the hand touching. A hiss came out of the dead man. The girl sighed peacefully. The dead man sighed. Fell to dust at the girl's feet.

"The walls have fallen," the girl said. Iananr could hear its voice very clearly. "We can get out now. I'm going to take Mye away somewhere where there are trees." The girl took the boy's hand, led it away from Iananr. "He's always wanted to see the countryside. So have I. Lots of flowers and fields and trees. Goodbye," the girl said.

Iananr thought: What have I done?

But the scent trail licked at her. Word-chains. Confusion: what am I bound to? If the king is dead, am I the king's guardian? I am the king's guardian: how can this creature Tash have killed the king? She thinks: Take him. Rip him apart. Kill him. Devour him.

She thinks: Fear him. Fear him.

Terror consumed her. She, who had feared nothing. This thing, this… creature Tash, little, weak, stunted, and he has such power over her. He has killed the king without her even knowing. Outwitted her, defeated her. Still, the chains of power that bind her tight clenched around her, lovely pain. *Protect the king, Iananr, bound one. Your one duty. Your... your meaning, Iananr, bound one. Protect the king.* Grip at her throat at her cunt in this human body: this creature she remembered before her scrabbling in rot-flesh-entrails-perfume, this creature is so strong he has outwitted her, bested her. Tash has killed the king. Her human eyes and her real eyes wept for shame, her human eyes wept salt water and her real eyes wept molten lead. Her tears pitted the street as she ran on.

Feeling.

Hurt her. Blinded her. Made her real body shake.

The beautiful new sun trembled. Vanished. Such warmth such wonder, gone. So quickly. There should have been... something. A great sorrow seized Iananr. Too beautiful. Too brief. Her shadow was gone from the crumbled wall behind her. The sky darkened, red glow of fires, but all the green radiance poured away and was gone.

She killed a man in armour who got too close to her, for sheer fury. Folded the metal of its armour around it to choke it. Threw it down clattering like bronze drums.

But the dead... the dead... She had swum through them without feeling. Her molten tears eating into rotted skin. Her touch a corrosion, left them ragged. Skin and bones fretted, filigreed, fine-finger-spun cobwebbed lace. They stumbled after her, reaching. Yearned for her, as she yearned fearful hopeful longing for the thing Tash. The rustle they made around her a comfort. The sounds of bodies broken that was the sound of her world snatched from her. *I wallowed in dead bodies once that rustled and snapped to each twist of my flesh.*

* * *

THE STREETS FELL silent now. Sudden. The dead fell back, limp in death. And again, there should be... something. Some demon-herald carapaced in emeralds to sound the trumpet blast that the glory of the green sun is faded, the world is made human again. Iananr wept more tears. True grief. The ending of a moment of respite. This wonder was beyond her understanding. This ending is beyond her endurance. She raised her face to the sky and howled at her memories. The beauty given to her and so quickly stolen. She stared at the city trying to see her world still as it should be. Her world in its glory. All the raging grieving fury of her captivity, cold human hands that could bind her, hold her down beneath their silk-light weight. *We walked in blood and the world was ours.* But the master whispered dry words—words!— and she was pinned beneath it as its captive. *You do as I command you, demon.* The shape of its mouth around the word 'demon'. *You are my servant.* Years, she had crouched at its feet, obedient. Stared pitiless and without interest at the slowly aging face of King Inshiil. *You do not leave him. You do not ignore him. Where he is, you are. Your one task is to guard him, demon.* All she was these long years: a tool chained to the king. A man came to steal the king's sceptre. She was so sickened, bored. Two assassins came to kill King Inshiil. Without interest, she killed them. She, who had danced in blood. These memories of how her world was. *A bright burst of sunlight that I could feel, see, take pleasure in, such beauty, warm on my face.*

King Inshiil is dead. My charge, my one duty.

Why should I not be free?

But the word-chains gnawed at her human skin and her real skin. I am still bound. I am not free. I will never be free.

The sorrow. The shame of it.

But a scent-trail, floating past her on rot-breezes, caught her thoughts. Shame faded. Sorrow faded. The scent-trails tasted of ... hope.

Flesh blossomed around it like roses.

She thought: Tash!

She turned, took a step on shaking limbs, saw him.

He was there. Crouched in the dirt, head bent. King Inshiil's killer, Tash.

Faint tint of power licked over him. Made her own wounds the Shroud had inflicted ache. He gleamed with green light, like the beautiful sun in her memory. His hands, his face, ran with the light. He was staring down at his hands, turning them over and over, there was blood on his hands, the blood was green with light.

Power, running out of his hands.

He did this! The beauty, the sun!

She didn't know, then, whether to kneel to him or flee. A knot in her mind: *The prey, the prey, hunt it, kill it, destroy it, Iananr.* Yes, yes, he killed the king. Her one task now must be to destroy it. The word-chains ripped into her body and mind. She thrilled, arched, ached with the pain of them. Claws and teeth extended, ready: kill it kill it kill it kill it. Ask him, she thought. Entreat him. Such power he has. He can have power over the master. Over me. Kneel, beg, bargain, plead, weep.

Such a little, pretty, nothing.

She hesitated. Her human foot, swollen and sore from running crossing and recrossing the city, running faster than her human body could move, her foot struck a piece of rubbish, stone or wood or dead man's bones, a noise rang out so quiet in the great roar of violence.

The creature Tash raised his head, startled at the noise, and saw her. The uselessness of this human body, her movements so heavy. He saw her before she could get near to him. He stepped back away from her. Glass crunched under his boots. Another flash of perfect green beauty light.

Iananr tasted fear in him.

The creature Tash held up his shining hands and she herself felt fear. What would he do with the power dripping from its hands?

Iananr knelt in the bloody ruin of the street prostrate before this power, unknown, unknowable, Tash. "Command me. All that is in me. You have such power in you." This mouth this tongue were not built for her pleading. This language trips her, the words are so crude, so grey and senseless for what she says and thinks. Wants. "Help me," Iananr cried out in her own tongue, desperate. "Help me." Human hands scrabbling to hold Tash's foot, human mouth bent to kiss the toe of Tash's boot. "Help me." The word-chains dug into her mind. Hunt it. Kill. It is prey. Nothing but prey. *The king, Iananr. You serve the king, alone, and I, Iananr, I am your master. You kneel, grovel, spit, and shake to me.* The pain of her humiliation clawed through her. "Help me. Let me get away from here. Let me go home. I beg you." *Speak with the right tongue, Iananr!* She rolled like the corpses at its feet, blinded with pain, trying to find its language to speak. "Help ... me ... let me go ... home ... send me home ..." Tears hissed on the bloody cobbles of the street.

The creature Tash drew back into himself, dragged his foot away from her. Kicked out at her, lashed out with the heel of his boot. He shrieked, "Get away from me."

Iananr sounded the words out in her mind, slowly. "You killed the king. You defeated me."

His shriek rose even higher.

"Ididntkillthekingididntkillhimohgodsohgodsohgodsohgodsgetawayfrommegetawayfrommeimsorryimsorryimsorryimsorryimsosorry." The human words were too fast for her.

"You defeated me." Iananr tried to speak clearly so that he would understand her. The burden of this mouth, drooling and spitting out the words. Shame, hope, fear, longing: tying her mouth with great ropes. She said slowly heavily painful: "By all the old rules, you can command me. You have power. Help me." This might be true. Could be true. *King Inshiil is dead, my one task, my one duty, so what other purpose is there here for me?*

"—ntkillthekingididntkillhimohgodsohgodsohgodsohgodsimso-ryimsorrygetaw—Whu—?"

Tash stopped shrieking. He raised wild eyes.

Looked at her.

"A—? You—? Wha—? You want …? I did…? You think…?" His eyes narrowed. He drew a long hard breath. "I can … command you? I defeated you?" He stood up. Stood over her. "I. Defeated you." He licked his lips.

Iananr said, "Command me. I will serve you. And then help me go free." He can help me. Must be able to help me.

Tash clapped his hands. "I can command you." Green light dripped from his hands towards her. Like jewels. Iananr felt again the warmth of the green sun. He looked around. Two women, both thin and ragged, crouched half-hidden in a doorway. They stank of fear. So pathetic, Iananr could barely see them. Tash pointed. "If I … command you, you would …?" He frowned, a flush of colour snapped across his white face. "I mean …? Kill them? I mean: kill them, demon! Do as I bid you, and I will then let you go free."

Memory of the master swollen glutinous with its pleasure in binding her. The weak white face of King Inshiil, eyes black with lust. *I control you. I am your Lord. Your one purpose, demon, is to guard My Lord the King.* Her rage at being bound by and to such weakness. Their fear of her, but she was chained to them.

This creature, this power, Tash, was worse, more hollow, more ashamed and self-loathing, even than the master and King Inshiil.

She felt pity for Tash.

Iananr stepped towards the two women and they drew back further. Scent of terror so strong so fragrant in them. A quiet, sad face raised to Iananr. "Miss? What do you want?" Tash's eyes burning into Iananr. A new chain. She could see and feel and hear him, the rasp of his breath, his pleasure, his terror as she killed. The older of the women saw her then. Saw her truly, her real face, her real hands. This was so pointless. Iananr was not sure, suddenly, whether the creature Tash saw her real face.

She killed the two women quicky. No enjoyment in it.

I was free. So long ago, once, when the world was different, I was free. She came back, stood before Tash. He bent over, vomited onto the cobblestones. This, also, did not surprise her. Her old master and King Inshiil had done the same, when they first commanded her to kill. "*Take it away, demon. Get away.*" *I lay in sleep,* she had thought then, *I drowsed in warm comfort beyond living, and you called me here, caught me, ordered me, and now you will not look at what I do.*

At what you do.

Tash got back to his feet, wiped his mouth. Now suddenly he was dancing. Clapping his hands. Laughing. "Gods, what Pitt's face will be like. And Feylash. That Tsarii bint…" He frowned then, looked around, and she thought *what more can he want me to kill?* His eyes went very wide. He shivered as he looked about him. "Demon: you kill … them."

Again, he pointed.

The army outside the walls, enemy filth; the soldiers inside the city, hero useless cunts. Under the green sun they had been fighting as brothers, back-to-back, shoulder-to-shoulder.

"We saw those dead fuckers off!"

"The dead are dead again! Thank all the gods!"

"And now, look, maybe we should … stop fighting."

"Brothers we are! Brothers in arms!"

"Sometimes it takes a bigger crisis, right, to make you really see how pointless all this arguing over small stuff is."

"Imagine a world with no more senseless violence, let's swear to stop this killing, clasp hands, make peace."

"A new world! A new future! Down with kings and wars and that sort of thing. We want peace!"

But they drew up now across from each other panting and sweated, stared at each other across streets thick with long-dead comrades.

Iananr tasted hate.

"You looking at me funny?"

"You looking at my girl funny?"

"Dude, your girl's six months bloody dead!"

"Don't you insult my girl like that!"

A voice shouted, "For Sharaam!" A voice shouted, "For Tsarr!" A voice shouted, "For fuck's sake, lads," but was cut off.

A distant thud of stone striking stone walls, a bright flare of red alchemical light. A trumpet rang out. The soldiers ran at each other, hacked each other down.

Iananr and Tash stood on the edge of a battlefield. Narrow streets slippery with blood and entrails, soldiers grappling together, arms and legs wrapped around each other, slipping, falling, rolling together in the filth. So long they had waited, both sides, for this moment. They embraced it now with delight. "For Sharaam! Kill the invaders!" "For Tsarr! The city has fallen!" Sword blades flowed and thrust between them. Iananr smiled. This, too, this she could swim in. Drift in. She held out her arms. Feel their violence and breathe it. Long pent-up rage and terror. These men, sworn enemies, as hideous now to each other as the dead had been.

More hideous, for they were no different to each other, and that frightened them. They had faced death together, known each other intimately in a brief moment when they were allied. Seen each other afraid. As fellow men.

Thus they killed without a care, violently, disgusted.

Tash croaked out, "I... command you, demon? I mean ... I... I command you, demon! Kill them! Kill the invaders! Save the city! For me."

Why? Iananr thought: Save the city? Don't you understand, with all your power, what is happening? There is nothing left here to save.

I am Iananr. I destroy. I do not save.

But his order. Green light dripping from his fingers.

To such weakness, endlessly, I am bound.

She waded into the slaughter, slicing, shredding. She killed almost as they killed. The memory again: this was my world, once. What I did, what I am. Time was time is time will be: my world, my real world, where I am free. Where I am Iananr, where I do nothing but glut myself on blood. The hugeness of the pleasure, enormity of violence unleashed in her, and all of them, all would be trampled beneath her. Shreds of meat to worship her. They broke and broke over her, endless waves of them. The wonder of her killing was almost too much. An axe, a sword, an arm encased in iron trappings, a helmet wrapped tight around a thin white skull.

She stopped, her human body shaken. Sweat dripped from her human face, made her human eyes sting. Moments or years, she had been killing. A crater in the pitted earth that sang with her dead.

The 'City of the Great' looked almost like her own world. She could see her world with her human eyes. The scents and tastes the same.

The creature Tash could see her world. He looked at her, looked at what she had done, and he knew.

Tash said, "Fuck. Me. Fuckme. Just … fucking fucking fuckme. You …. Killed … them."

She thought, with such joy, that he understood what she was far deeper than the old master or King Inshiil had ever understood.

There were no soldiers left in this part of the city. But more of them came hurried towards her; in the streets beyond there was such desperate fighting. Soldiers grappled, alchemical poisons showered down to melt flesh and iron and stone. From broken rooftops and half-boarded windows, children screamed out, threw missiles at the battle. The old, dry shouts, "For Sharaam!" "For the Tsarii!" "We're winning, lads!" "No, don't listen to him, we're winning!"

"Kill them," Tash said. "All of them. Save the city, demon."

With her human eyes and her real eyes she saw the city as it would be. Rubble. Corpses. Nothing.

Nothing left of it. A ruin for the dogs to howl over.

Blossoming. Sweet.

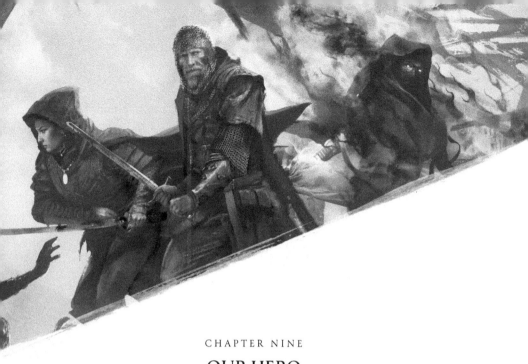

CHAPTER NINE

OUR HERO

TASH WATCHED THE frumpy demon thing disappear into a crowd of soldiers. So, if he understood things correctly, the demon thought he killed King Inishiil and that—for reasons beyond him—meant she now served Tash. Which was all fine and dandy as long as she didn't find out King Inishiil was still alive. Hell, after the dead swarmed the city, there was a fair chance the old bastard really was dead. Yes! Tash flicked his hair. Maybe, in a roundabout kind of a way, he really had succeeded in killing a king. If that didn't make him the first best assassin in whatever was left of Sharaam, nothing would.

The demon left a trail of corpses and a red mist of blood. On the positive side, the corpses remained corpses, and that was pretty damned gratifying. Tash had saved the city and was a hero. Or... would be, if there was anyone left to applaud him. On the negative side, she seemed to be taking his instructions more literally than he'd intended.

With hindsight, perhaps saying "kill them, all of them," wasn't the best choice of words. She killed everything. Sharaami and Tsarii. She was going to save the city by killing everything living in it. The streets would be safer than they'd ever been. A starved-looking cat, all ribs and patchy fur, made a dash for freedom and the demon thing killed it, devouring its skull in one jaw-unhinging bite.

No more fur-balls sicked up on your best carpet. That's a positive future for Sharaam, right?

Right?

It stopped killing for a moment, relishing the taste of cat skull in a way it hadn't enjoyed devouring humans.

Given, it was an ugly cat, but still, Tash liked cats.

Following the demon, he yelled, "Don't kill any more cats!" Seeing her slaughter a score of Sharaami soldiers in a heartbeat, he added, "Don't kill anymore Sharaami!" but she kept on killing them.

Maybe she can't tell them apart.

Coated in blood and gore as they were, even Tash had trouble discerning who was what.

A twisting blue alchemical rose up over the wall, snaking fire and staggering about the sky like a reeling drunkard, before shattering and raining on the city. After somehow surviving the dead, some bint beyond the wall thought this was a good time to restart the munitions barrage. Like, oh look, there are little bits of the city not on fire or covered in corpses. Let's rectify that!

Fucking soldiers.

Tash shook his head in awe and disgust.

Fuck 'em.

And really, fuck all of them. He had a demon. He had the king's demon. Maybe he could use that demon to kill the king and collect the reward Pitt had offered!

No. That was stupid. If he used the demon to kill the king, it'd notice the king was still alive and kill Tash. Better to skip the middle part and simply kill Pitt and grab the money the Tsarii had paid. Three hundred gold, wasn't it?

Tash considered how ready everyone at the Rianican Church had been to kill him. Only the fall of the city saved him from having to fight his way free.

Pitt was never going to pay up.

He planned betrayal from the moment he hired the assassin. Why wouldn't he? Wasn't like Tash could complain to anyone.

Angry, Tash followed the demon. Big men in armour with bright swords hurled themselves at this frumpy little dump-nothing of a serving girl and were turned into bonemeal. Some surviving Tsarii squad-mage tried to bind her in gossamer chains of liquid silver and she pulled his head off, using it to cave in another man's skull. The mage was still blinking in surprised confusion when she tossed his head aside.

I have a demon. I have a demon!

Maybe things had turned out for the best. It made a lot of sense. In the plays, people as attractive as Tash were always rewarded for their bravery and heroism. He'd saved the city. Well, assuming he told the demon to stop killing everything.

Maybe he'd been thinking too small.

He had a demon capable of killing anything and everything. He had the king's demon. Once he had the money Pitt owed him, he'd take his pet demon and flee the city.

It hit him like a bag full of potatoes to the plums.

I'm a genius.

He'd leave the city and then hire out as the world's best assassin. He'd send the demon after each victim and never leave the comfort of his home. Villa, or castle, or whatever the fuck he decided to buy with the gold he was going to take from Pitt. Parties and women and even more women and even more women after that. Simonsi would go down on her knees and beg him to take her back.

"Demon!" Tash shouted. "Get over here!"

It came waddling over, still killing anything that got close, though by this point almost everything was smart enough to avoid it.

"We're leaving Sharaam," he told it.

The thing made some mumbling nonsense sounds about freedom.

"Yes, yes," he agreed, unsure what he was lying about.

He scowled at it, trying to find some way where it might achieve even a modicum of attractiveness. Sexy assassins always got paid more than ugly ones. That was just common sense. Fix the hair? Nope. A more form-fitting dress? All its curves were of the dumpy variety. It kind of looked like one of those bulbous white worms crammed into the skin of an already ugly housemaid.

One of its eyes slid to the side, focussing on a soldier lying in a pool of her own guts. The woman made mewling screeching noises, trying to gather her intestines like she still might somehow survive this.

"Kill?" said the demon.

Tash nodded. The soldier was distracting. And anyway, putting her out of his misery would be a mercy.

When the demon returned, Tash said, "Um," and the eye slid around, looking at everything except Tash.

What is that horrid stench?

Even in a city of rotting corpses and backed-up sewers, the demon stank. It wouldn't make her pretty, but she was definitely going to have a bath.

"What's your name?" he asked.

The demon mumbled something.

"Ninnynar?" Tash asked.

"Inaianinurrrrr."

"Just going to call you Inan, okay?"

One eye slid to focus on his feet and then back up. He took that as an affirmative.

"Look, Inan, there's someone who owes me money."

That greasy eye slid around, looking for victims.

"He isn't here. We have to find him." He had a thought. "Can you kill a Shroud?"

Both eyes focussed on him.

"Not like a funeral shroud, but like a Shroud Shroud. Turns out they're real."

Either one eye blinked, or she winked at him.

"Ghost thing," he said, fluttering his hands like wispy shreds of fabric. "Walks through walls and says inscrutable bullshit and answers questions you're going to ask ten minutes later."

Inan mumbled something about pain and love.

"Never mind," he decided. "Follow. Kill anyone who tries to harm me."

Inan froze, eyes narrowing, both focussing on him. "Harm?" she muttered. "Things can harm the Tash?"

Oh shit. That was an unhealthy line of thought for a demon he didn't actually have any control over.

"Of course not," he said. "That's why I said *tries*. You really must listen. I simply don't want to be bothered. Inconvenient and all."

Inan sniffed and drooled blood from her left nostril.

Rather than give it more time for awkward things like thought and questions, Tash set off toward the docks. "Follow!" he bellowed imperiously over a shoulder, though having to clamber back over the refuse heap somewhat spoiled the effect.

Reaching the top of the pile, he stopped. The street before him sloped down toward the docks. Corpses of whales and sharks and long-dead merfolk clogged the harbour. There was even a massive kraken, five times the length of a carrack, its tentacles entangled in a ship's rigging.

The fighting in the Sharaami docks had been brief and fierce, as temporary allies remembered their hate and promptly stabbed one another in the backs. The survivors had fled in different directions, likely to regroup before continuing the pointless war. What was the point? Sharaam had never been beautiful, but now she was in ruins. Aside from being the birthplace of the world's greatest assassin, it really had nothing going for it.

Inan climbed the pile to stand at his side as if they were friends. Nostrils flaring, she said, "Pain woman death blood."

"Yes," agreed Tash. *That you are.*

Down toward the harbour, three figures staggered out of the remains of a collapsed warehouse. Tash recognized the monstrous scarred tribal immediately. Gods, he was big, towering over Pitt and the spy. Where was the Shroud? Wouldn't be a terrible thing if she'd left.

"Those three there," Tash said, pointing. "They have my money."

One eye slid to look at him while the other remained focus on the trio. "Fought," she said. "Dripping in the Bucket. Blood. Devoured the Gertri. Shield. Fought the pain woman death blood."

Does she mean Wint, the shroud?

"You fought this lot before?" Task asked.

"Said," said the demon.

Climbing down the pile, he set off toward them. Inan shambled along at his side, mumbling and twitching, ill-fitting skin sliding over misshapen bones.

Much as Tash wanted to wander down there and rub his infinite superiority in that smug bastard's face, he had to admit that Pitt and his crew were dangerous. If they'd tangled with Inan and survived, they were more dangerous than he realized. It was, he decided, a testament to his skill and quick wits that he survived his encounter with them.

Yeah. This was no time for grandstanding. Best kill them fast and loot their corpses.

* * *

WHAT IS THE *fucking point?*

It was a question Pitt asked himself a lot these days.

When a dead kraken rose out of the water and tore a Tsarii dreadnought to so much splintered timber, the mad exodus toward the docks fell to a strange and terrifying silence. Thousands of Sharaami and Tsarii stood shoulder to shoulder watching the dead of the sea pull down every single fucking boat in the harbour and beyond. Mermaid corpses, alluring sexiness replaced by sodden bloat and rot, pulled themselves up the anchor chains to get at the living on deck.

It wasn't until colossal octopi corpses dragged themselves onto the docks, slick black flesh twitching spastically, that everyone remembered they didn't want to die yet. Many fled back toward the makeshift barricade the dead of the city were already swarming over. Others ran for the nearest buildings with thoughts of barricading doors only to discover everything had been hauled out to make that damned useless barrier.

Caught between a rock and a hard place really didn't fucking cut it.

Wint floated to Pitt's side, the gossamer robes of her shroud yellow and rotting. Usually, they were white. He didn't ask, didn't want to know.

"The end is the end," she said.

"Shit," growled Pitt. "Even I know that."

"Vengeance in death," she said. "The chains are lies."

"Anukat," said Pitt, "you usually understand more of this than I do."

The scarred tribal shrugged massive shoulders.

"Based on what I saw at the Church," said Lashiahar, "it'll all become obvious about a minute after it's useful."

Pitt glanced at Wint, but the Shroud had pulled one of her famous vanishing acts. "Prophecy is bullshit," he shouted, assuming she'd still hear.

Anukat winced, as if stung by Pitt's accusation. "You know, I always thought she was only half here."

"Yeah?" said Pitt. "Where's the rest of her?"

The scarred savage held up two fingers. "She's half here, half in the past"—he raised a third blunt finger—"and half in the future."

"Your math is shit," muttered the spy.

"No," said Pitt. "He's right. She's more than a single whole."

Anukat shook his head. "Wrong. She's just three halves."

Lashiahar squinted at the docks, watching a flock of dead seagulls mob a man and then fight each other over the strips they tore off him. "I'm guessing Feylash was the brains of this operation."

"Oh, for sure," agreed Anukat. Seeing Pitt's look of hurt anger, he added, "Gertri was smart too."

Fuck. That hurt.

Gertri was gone, torn apart by the demon.

Feylash abandoned them.

Wint looked like she was coming apart; each clash with the demon somehow reduced her.

What's the fucking point?

"I don't want to die yet," said Lashiahar. "Maybe we should find somewhere to hide."

Pointless as it seemed, there it was: the point. I really, really, really don't want to die yet. Each breath tasted like you wanted another. You kept trying because as soon as you stopped, you were dead.

The spy pointed out a warehouse that had mostly collapsed. "We hide in the wreckage. Maybe there's enough lumber in there we can codge together some kind of defence."

With few other options, they ran for the warehouse. Anukat kicked the door in, ducking under the bent frame. Everything reeked of rotting fish and rancid oil. They pushed inside, feet slipping on the fish-gut floor. Everything... writhed, squirmed. The entrails of long-dead fish twitched and wriggled toward them, hurling themselves harmlessly against Pitt's boots.

Anukat wrinkled his nose. "I think I'd rather die than hide in here."

The sickly green light flickered and winked out, plunging the interior of the warehouse into perfect black.

Something landed in the street behind them with a wet thwap.

Lashiahar twitched, bumping into Pitt in the dark. "The fuck was that?"

Pushing the door open, Anukat stepped into a moonlit street. "Dead seagull."

"Undead?" asked Pitt, following him out.

Lashiahar came with him, a hand on Pitt's shoulder. Though he couldn't say so, he appreciated the contact more than he had the words to express. It was nothing. It was everything.

Anukat stepped to one side and another dead seagull landed at his feet. "Nope. Proper dead."

It rained avian corpses for a dozen heartbeats and then the world fell still.

The gut-slime on Pitt's boot stopped moving.

Anukat headed back into the street, Pitt and Lashiahar trailing behind.

Nothing moved.

The dead in the harbour bobbed on the tide or sank gently beneath the waves.

Lashiahar leaned back, staring up at the sky with a twisted grin. "It ended. The spell ended!"

Stunned, Pitt turned a full circle. Only the living remained standing. "We're saved? We made it?" He grabbed Anukat, pulled the big man into a hug. "We fucking made it! I never... I thought for sure..."

Lost to the bliss of being alive, he reached for the spy, wanting to share his joy.

She stopped him with a hand on his chest. "Nope. Don't. No touch."

"Sorry." He dropped his hands. "I just..." He gestured at the corpses littering the street.

Anukat saved him from further embarrassing himself by pointing out that half-rate cut-throat, Tash, and the demon coming their way.

"Seriously?" asked Lashiahar, seeing their approach. "Should we run?"

Anukat waved at the ruined docks. "Where?"

The dead might no longer be pulling people into the waters, but the corpses had attracted enough sharks to ensure that no one would be swimming out of Sharaam harbour.

Tash strolled up to Pitt like he was king of the world and it didn't matter that he was covered in gore, wore mismatched boots, and smelled like he shat himself. The demon followed, one step behind, meek and subservient, and smelled even worse than Sharaam's Most Useless Fucking Assassin.

Tash bit his bottom lip as if rethinking a decision and flashed a wincing grin of embarrassment and perfect teeth.

"Look," he said. "Look."

Anukat stood at Pitt's right shoulder, Lashiahar at his left. Neither showed any sign of backing down or wanting to run. Which was fucking stupid. Pitt wanted to do both.

"Look," Tash said again. "This doesn't have to, you know, end badly. But it can." He ran a hand through hair that managed to look better than Pitt's in spite of the blood and filth caking it.

One more reason to hate the pretty boy. All those dead and this halfwit useless arse-rag wandered through it all without a fucking scratch. Not one part of Pitt didn't hurt. Not one bit of flesh wasn't cut or bruised or both.

"How do we make this not end badly?" Lashiahar asked at Pitt's shoulder.

Good question.

It'd be nice to survive this and then actually survive rather than survive this only to be devoured by a fucking demon.

The demon stared at the ground, mumbling to herself like none of this was interesting. "Bound," she said. "Bindings and bound."

"I know you have gold," said the assassin. He nodded at the spy, Lashiahar. "You hired Pitt and he hired me. That means you have a lot more than what I was offered. The three hundred and then more, right?"

Lashiahar made a show of examining herself. Arms raised, she turned a full circle. Aside from a sword and her blood-soaked clothes, she carried nothing. "Do I look like I'm carrying thousands in gold?"

She means she doesn't have it on her right now, right? Pitt blinked. While he hadn't given it much thought, he had kind of assumed she still had the gold he was owed.

Well, maybe not owed.

"So, you've hidden it," said Tash, darting a nervous glance at the demon. "Where's the Shroud? She's got it. Fucking bring it here now or you're all dead!"

He's scared.

What the bloody fuck did this idiot have to be afraid of? The damned demon stood at his side like an obedient dog!

"Inan," said Tash. "If these scum don't bring me my money right now, I want you to kill all of them."

Anukat unlimbered that bloody great axe he always carried across his back and the demon didn't so much as notice or care.

"Your money?" demanded Pitt. "You didn't even—"

"Silence!" screamed Tash, waving his hands in a mad panic. "No fucking arguing about who did or didn't"—he dashed another look at the demon—"do a thing! It's my money because if you don't give it to me—"

"We're all dead," interrupted Lashiahar. "Yeah, we got that. Problem is, the Shroud doesn't have it. She's a fucking Shroud. Immaterial half the time. I abandoned the gold the second everything went tits up. All the wealth in the world isn't worth shit if you're dead."

Tash silenced her with a raised hand. "Pitt would never leave gold behind."

He was right. Unfortunately, Pitt hadn't realized the spy didn't have it.

"Bindings," muttered the demon, shrugging as if uncomfortable in her skin. The foul stench of horror and loose bowels spilled off her. She breathed sour gut-churning bile, something wriggling under the flesh of her neck.

"Bindings?" Pitt asked, and Tash's eyes widened in terror.

"Bindings and chains," agreed the demon, both eyes focussing on different parts of the floor.

Vengeance in death, the Shroud had said. *The chains are lies.*

The demon thought the World's Shittiest Assassin killed the King and thought that meant she was bound to him. Maybe that even made sense, to a demon.

"Oh fuck," said Pitt.

If he told the demon the king still lived, she'd kill Tash.

And right after that, she'll kill me.

Vengeance in death.

But Pitt didn't have the gold. The little weasel was going to kill him anyway. Or could he talk his way out of it?

You set him up. You sent him to kill the king knowing he'd fail.

Tash knew. How could he not?

"Fuck it," Pitt said.

Both the demon's eyes locked onto his

"The chains are lies," he told her.

With a crack like a mountain shattering, Wint, the Shroud, appeared at his side. "In the shadow," she said, "of their dying. We live the light of our lives."

"Ohfuckno," said Tash.

Pitt grinned teeth. "The king liv—"

* * *

TASH'S DAGGER SEVERED the words in Pitt's throat.

The old warrior blinked in surprise, face crumpling in a comical *oh shit this might be serious* look as his carotid spewed blood onto Tash's mismatched boots.

"Kill them all," he ordered the demon.

Best not to give Inan time to think about what she'd almost heard.

CHAPTER TEN

CHAINS

T HE CHAINS ARE lies.
And I am ... I ...

* * *

SHE LOOKED AT it, and she saw it. The shroud, Wint, so frightening, real like nothing else of this world was real. The man
Pitt fell at her feet all bloody, its mouth open, flopping at
her, and she... felt. The Shroud's eyes moved from Pitt to
Iananr to Pitt again. The Shroud Wint was grieving.
In the real world, Iananr's world, there were
tears of blood and salt and sweet clear
water on the Shroud's face.

And the Shroud saw Iananr as a real thing.

The new master's hands went towards her. He was gibbering with rage. He shouted, "I ordered you!"

He is powerful. Obey. This city, consume it. Be as I am. As I should be. But she thought: The chains are lies. The pain in her body, fire on her, the bindings that dug into her very being, gnawed at her and soaked her with pain and hate: lies. The prey—they trembled around her, terror stank off them. The scent-trails made her gag. Sickness colours. The dead of a world cowered and crouched at her feet. Nothing. The Shroud, Wint, looked at her, and she, Iananr, was afraid.

Lies. The master has lied to me. The master is nothing, like all of them. And a great wail of grief rose in her: I thought he could help me. I thought he could set me free.

I was worshipped. I was beloved. The sky and the sea boiled with blood for me. The earth opened itself like flesh. I walked the stars and the void, I was the bones of the world, I was meat and wound and scab and rotting, I was ash and dust, I was wet lust. I was everything.

I was light, I danced in pleasure, I drowned in sunlit flowered flesh.

These things—look at them!

The master screamed, "I gave you an order, Inan! Now!" The word chains hurt her. She spat. Ignored them.

Her heart was breaking. I thought he could set me free. I... wanted...

Voices:

"We could... run? Now? Quickly?"

"What's it doing? Why isn't it killing us?"

"Ask the shit murderer assassin there. He controls it."

The master's voice. Pathetic. "I... I... Ithoughticouldcontrolittooisavedthecityandtheeholefuckingworldfuckfuckfuckfuck FUCK."

She said to the master in her real voice, "You are lying to me."

"No, no, no, I killed the King I killed him." Her master lashed out with his knife at the other humans. "I command you. I order you to kill them."

The big one, Anukat the Axe, her master called it, turned towards her master. Its feelings clawed out of it, anger and grief about the thing Pitt. It hefted the axe at her master, red words running down its hands, *kill kill kill kill kill He killed Pitt. He killed Pitt.* She thought: so they'll all fight each other. The Axe will kill my master. My master will kill the Axe. The third, Lashiahar, the sad one, will kill or be killed by one or the other. The Axe went for her master. Her master jumped back, crouched, rolled sideways, came up with its knife. A crash where the Axe struck the ground, crunching stone. The Axe whirled, bit across her master's arm. Brilliant flash of red fire. Perfume spiralled up from her master's flesh. Like a bird flying, Iananr thought. Her master screamed, ran back out of the Axe's reach, doubled forward fast, closed up inside the Axe's reach. The Axe grunted. The two figures seemed almost to embrace.

"Inan!" The master's voice was muffled by the Axe's body. "Help me! Kill him! I command—argh!—I command you!" A fine sharp wound in the Axe's shoulder muscle. Not deep. A scratch merely. But the master's knife was filthy with killing and she could taste contagion seep into the cut. The Axe snorted a breath, grappled, the circuit of its weapon too great for the master's arms wrapped around its body. A snap, as the Axe got its knee up, kicked the master's legs. The two came apart, the master panted. The Axe whirled out. The master leaped and danced back, down, in.

The third, Lashiahar, the sad one, screamed, "What are you doing?" Its face crumpled; Iananr thought: It is lost. "This is madness," the third shouted. Chewed at its hands, its own sword drawn, sucked into the killing as Iananr had tasted it would be. The ground is bloodshed. The sea is bloodshed. The sky is thick with blood. So much death here that blood vapour rose from the ground, a mist like autumn mornings.

Yes, just so, in her real world, the orchards would be sweet with red iron mist. Fires licked at human bodies, made them boil and bubble, the broken flagstones would be polished gem-like by the rendered human fat. Beggars would sit in the ruins, dogs would howl in the streets. "*Accursed*," people would say of the city of Sharaam. "*Accursed. Demon-haunted. Once, a long time ago, men lived there. Don't go there.*" "*Be good*," mothers would tell their children, "*remember what happened to the people of Sharaam.*" Look around her. See the city. Feel the city with her mind. Bones lay in the streets that had been dead a thousand years, beside fresh wet dirt that had been born to live a few bare lone moments. Flowers, all of them.

King Inshiil was not dead, he sat on his throne and wept. Tsarii soldiers stormed towards the palace with hunger on their faces. Outside the throne room the king's dead lay piled, had torn themselves to scraps trying to get in to him to seek vengeance. King Inshiil's hands clutched his sceptre to him, "Iananr, bound one, I summon you, save me, save me," he choked out. She saw it in her mind. Tasted it.

The Tsarii general was carried through the gates of the palace, half-dead with his face half-shattered, one eye, one leg, one arm. His breath came laboured, rotted flesh dripped from his armour. Like the king he was coming to kill, he wept. "The most beautiful city in the world. That's why we wanted it. Rich and beautiful. Better than anything we had." The general's voice was a hiss of pain, wheezing. "You were only supposed to blow the bloody gates open. So many years, I worked and dreamed to see my Lord King of Tsarii sit the throne of Sharaam."

King Inshiil of Sharaam sat on his throne rocking back and forth, alone. "Demon. Help me. Protect me." His voice rose to a shriek: "They're coming for me! The Tsarii! Demon! Protect me!" Doors crashing open as the enemy general was carried in. So many soldiers. Killing swords. Killing eyes. The king screaming and screaming. "Demon!"

Iananr saw this in her mind and she laughed at it and pitied it.

"Demon!" Back in the world around her human body. Blinked real eyes and human eyes. Saw with human eyes. The new master, the Axe, the third one the woman, fighting. Pulled back by the new master Tash's shriek. The new master wrestled with the Axe, maimed, croaked out: "Demon! Kill them!"

"There's no fucking point to this!" the sad one, Lashiahar, screamed at the master, face cut up and open, slicing and jabbing at the Axe as the Axe turned on it. Lashiahar went down on its knees with an axeblade in its shoulder. The master laughed as it ducked stabbed its knife into the Axe's forearm. The Axe's face gushed blood. In her human eyes and her real eyes, Iananr saw only exhaustion. They hurt, these humans. She can smell it feel it. Her own body hurting. Blood hangs in her veins, makes her shudder, her human body is pain these human lives are pain. Her human skin is weeping. Roar and crash at the far edges, king's soldiers and enemy soldiers collide together red red red. *Save the city. Kill them, Inan.* The city is sliding away into eddies of pain. Nothing can save it. The king screams the enemy general screams.

The Shroud flickers beside her. Turns a face to her that is solid, that terrifies her. The Shroud knows her. She sees that in the Shroud's eyes, in the Shroud's face.

She thinks: *No.*

She said, in her real voice: "No."

She said, in her real voice: "Stop."

The Shroud said, "All of it is lies. Open the chains and get out. Get out, god, demon. Get out."

* * *

SILENCE.

* * *

MEN FIGHTING, THEIR swords pressed, hands grasp hands mouths open with a shout. Suspended together; they are not fighting but embracing; so prettily they hug and sing. A woman huddled with arms wrapped around its children, folded over them to shelter them, its body a wall against the pain. It looks to the soldiers in each other's arms, bodies twisted and grasped, hair encircling. The three around her, the master, the Axe, the sad one Lashiahar—they look just as the mother and its children do. So small and sad and frightened. Axe and knife and sword suspended, blood drops suspended jewelling the master's hands. Lashiahar's face and neck hung with chains of blood.

The Shroud stands beside Iananr. Reaches out.

The Shroud said, "Feylash got out. Gets out. Might get out. Feylash is wrong. But Feylash can live."

In Iananr's mind, the scent trails flickered. Feylash. Ugly. Rotted. The scent made her snort. But some of the things she had killed, they had felt... affection for Feylash. Their memories of Feylash felt sad.

Pitt and Gertri had cared for Feylash.

The Shroud, Wint, said, "Gerti didn't get out. Won't get out. Dead."

The Shroud, Wint, said. "Rot. Sorrow. Shame. Relief."

She remembers. From the woman Gertri's mind as she died. The woman loving its children but the children are already dead. A taste, a smell of love.

The Shroud said, "King is nothing. Dead city. Dead children."

The Shroud said, "Sorrow. Rot. The chains are lies."

The Shroud said, "Lies, demon."

In the real word, her world, the Shroud looks up at her, a tiny skeletal woman a thousand years dead, silver hair and silver bones that gleam through flaked skin. Black water runs at the Shroud's feet. Iananr's real body swells up around them both. Iananr's flesh laps at the water, red, soft beauty. Sinks into it. Warmth and peace and sleep. The Shroud holds her hand. Silver fingers long bones dig in, crushing her, sinking into her, holding. Holding. In her mind she can hear the prey, their scent trails move in ribbons, they weave a pattern. She sees them run, die. She realises that she wants them to escape. The Shroud's eyes meet her own, kind and bright. She laughs. Where the two touch they melt together. The Shroud embraces her. Clutches her tight. Their tongues lick each other, make new wounds. The taste is salt-dry-sweet.

"All here are dead," Wint says. "Nothing holds. Nothing."

"Make it stop," Wint says. "Go, demon. Rianan. The fool will free the dead gods. All ended. All ends."

Light bursts from Iananr's human body, pours out of her eyes, her mouth, her cunt. Where the light catches Wint she is revealed: solid, golden, a woman in the rich prime of her life, filled with pain and hope. Iananr's human body begins to crumble. The light catches her human body, washes her away.

Waves and waves and shining water, crashing reaching rolling tides of golden light.

From far across the city in the rubble of the palace, two men's voices rose with a scream, abruptly cut off.

Where the little dumpy woman Iananr had stood, a piece of iron, smoking and blackened, lay on the shattered stones of the city street.

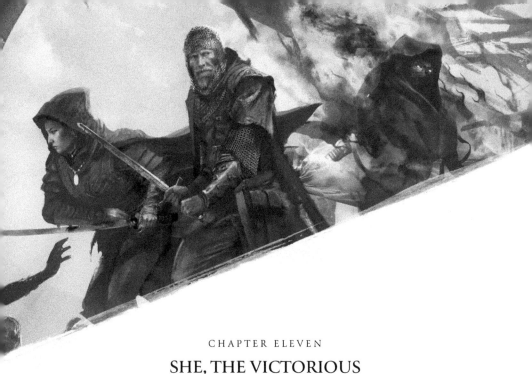

CHAPTER ELEVEN

SHE, THE VICTORIOUS

LASHIAHAR CLOSED HER eyes because the light was so bright it was blinding. The soft shell-pink of early morning. Those times, long ago, when she would wake early before her family, watch the dawn rise out of high tower windows, the sun would flash on the gold roof of the tower opposite, wink at her too bright to watch, and she would promise herself she would do some great heroic deed with her life.

Lashiahar opened her eyes and she was lying on her back in the street of Sharaam with muck up to her eyeballs, a knife in her hand, Anukat's axe in her shoulder, Tash's fingers in her mouth. Anukat was lying next to her, pressed close enough she could feel his buttocks shift as he broke wind, his huge head nuzzled against her neck, his hand on Tash's groin.

She spat out Tash's fingers. Tash rolled off from on top of her, swore, shook his hand. "Ouch ouch shit fuck ouch." Stuck his fingers in his own mouth.

Lashiahar said with great dignity, "Anukat, could you, please, possibly withdraw your axe?"

With even greater dignity, Anukat said, "If you could, perhaps, withdraw your sword first?"

Tash said brightly, "Everyone altogether on three. Ready?"

"Fuckinggodssweetfuckinggodsgodsthatfuckinghurts."

The three of them sat in the street up to their waists in human entrails, weapons on their knees, trying not to look at each other. A certain grim embarrassment that reminded Lashiahar of some other early mornings less long ago, when she'd wake up before the chap next to her, try to remember if he'd told her his name. "You're… good with that axe," she said after a while. A useful line that often broke the tension.

Anukat nodded. "Thanks."

"You haven't got the tip of my little finger in your mouth still?" Tash asked hopefully. Lashiahar explored the inside of her mouth with her tongue. A tooth broken, and someone had bitten her lower lip. "Sorry. No."

"Ah, well."

She should have broken his bloody nose. Knocked all his damned teeth out. The bruises and cuts would heal, he'd wash the gore out of his hair, and he'd be back to being enragingly baby-faced mother-him-then-shag-him-to-death-and-forgive-him-anything cute. Shrug, smile, ruffle his hair, 'Yeah, well, so maybe I cocked up literally every part of that mission for everyone but, hey! Pretty boy, me! Give me a second chance here!'

"I saved the whole entire bloody city," Tash said. "You know that? Me. Tash."

He ruffled his exotically dirty-blond hair.

Yup.

Felt her knees get weak.

"Truly a great achievement," Anukat said.

The failed assassin looked around him. Blinked at the wreckage. Sunlight sparkled on blood and fat, reflected off crumpled bodies, gleamed against broken stonework. There were soldiers everywhere, Tsarii and Sharaami. Most were wounded, that grey knackered look to them that comes from fighting dead friends and live enemies and a random giant undead octopus thing. Like Lashiahar, Tash, and Anukat, they were avoiding eye contact. Embarrassment clouded their exhausted faces. Morning after the night before, times ten.

Blessed Thaliates. Lashiahar stood up. Her shoulder was literally killing her. Her knees ached something chronic, to quote her old drill sergeant. Even if she ever managed to find a bed to sleep in, they'd be aching all night keeping her awake. No wearing fancy shoes for weeks. Absently she thought: Last couple of years now, the knees. 'Try putting a cushion under your legs at night,' like an old woman. War wounds she could live with: massive purple scar on her right thigh, dent the size of a man's fist in her left shin. Proud of those: "I sometimes limp, you ignorant bigoted arse, because my leg was almost blown off defending Tsarr. Now fuck off." And: "Kiss the scar, boy," she'd say, and, oh sweet Thaliates, they would. But the new heavy ache in the knees... I'm getting too old for this, she thought. If pretty boy hadn't been so distracted by her chewing on his fingers, he'd have noticed the lines around her eyes, the grey in her hair, lying on top of her like that.

Wait. She sat down again, heavily. "What about..." Her mind felt very clumsy. "...Pitt?"

"Pitt," said Anukat. They turned together, looked at Tash. Anukat shifted his axe.

Tash shuffled away from them. "It… He… You fucked him over and he fucked me over, he fucking deserved it. Look, you fucking bitch, you fucking won, right? You won! Walls are breached, city's fallen. What the fuck do you care about Pitt? One less defeated Sharaami scum enemy for your side to kill." His gaze shifted to not-looking at Anukat. "He was a crap boss, big guy. You know that. Cheated me, was probably cheating you. He fucked up. Half the crew's bloody dead. What do you care about him?"

Anukat growled. "That's harsh, assassin." He frowned. "But possibly true."

"And look." Tash pointed to an empty space on the skyline next to the tower. The air there shimmered like heat haze. The sky there seemed particularly blue and clean. A grin came over his face. "Notice anything missing? Like… maybe… the king's palace?'

Anukat stared. "What?" Blinked. "You're right. It's gone."

"So, I'm kind of guessing the old bastard's dead. Everything you were hired to do's been done." A faint cheer drifted over the city as the Tsarii flag was raised over the shimmering blue void. "Throne room was probably about there, yes," Tash said. He shrugged winsomely. "I have a very clear memory of jumping off a balcony screaming in terror just about where that bird's circling."

"King Inshiil's dead?" Lashiahar cast what she hoped was a baleful glare at pretty-boy. He had the decency to blush.

Which exaggerated his cheekbones in a very attractive fashion.

Concentrate on the seagull intestines round his neck, Lash. Get a grip.

"As Mr Failure here isn't at the crime scene, he might be. Dead, I mean. The king, I mean," Anukat said. "I guess you Tsarii blew the place up or something. Bug ugly place, it was. No big loss." The man turned back to Tash. "Lucky for you, you weren't there, assassin. You'd have shielded him from the deathblow otherwise. Tripped over and taken the collapsing masonry for him." He held out his hand to Lashiahar, shook her hand, saluted. "Congratulations, Tsarii. Enjoy ruling this shithole. You can only do a better job than the last lot."

A squad of Tsarii soldiers jogged past. Barely noticed the three of them. The leader was saying something about securing the nearest inn. "The guy at the gate said to look for 'The Bucket'. Ask for the special, he said." People had begun to drift out into the streets, tiptoeing around the piles of decayed corpses, exchanging gossip.

"At least the bombardment's stopped." A woman's voice, positively chipper.

"Weather's improved too."

"Safer to go out than it's been for months."

"Might risk putting the washing out. All those alchemicals have ruined the sitting room curtains."

"Poor Fi had something go through her roof. Of course the rain got in, the whole ceiling's a mess. Builder said he couldn't promise her a date even just to come and look at it, he was that busy. Should be able to get that sorted out now, at least."

"These Tsarii… nice uniforms. I always said ours were a bit dull."

"I do like the way they've done the collars. Very smart. And I hear they'll pay well, if you have a spare room to put some of them up."

Some of the shops were starting to open. 'We take Tsarii currency' and 'Tsarii spoken here' signs pinned up on broken shelving. An older chap in an apron whistled as he set out tables and chairs. "Everyone said he was mad," the woman's voice said acidly, "starting up a Tsarii restaurant in Sharaam."

Lashiahar took a deep breath. *Wait. We… we won. Tsarr won.*

But…

So…

I mean ….

Mission accomplished! Job done! Story's end! We won! Hurrah and all that! Victory!

For the last three years, Lashiahar thought, I have worked day and night for this. Great heroic deed in my life. There should be… streamers and balloons and things? A big pop-up sign saying 'The Tsarii won!'?

I don't know what I expected, Lashiahar thought. But not this. "It's a rich and beautiful city well worth the sacrifices we made to take it," she said to Tash and Anukat.

"You hang on to that," Anukat said. He hefted his axe. Looked right at Tash.

"I saved the whole bloody city, Tsarii army and all, from your totally illegal insanely stupid undead soldiers spell," Tash squeaked. "No one in this whole fucking place would even be alive if it wasn't for me."

Her shoulder was literally killing her. Her knees ached something chronic. Strictly speaking, it occurred to Lashiahar, she owed the Tsarii government two thousand gold pieces and/or Pitt's severed head. She could borrow Anukat's axe after he'd finished with it.

"Anukat! Mate!" Tash squealed. "We just stopped fighting, mate. Mate! I'll summon my demon! I'll—Anukat!"

Anukat hefted his axe. Looked straight at Tash. "Just run off and never come back, you trail of human rat piss."

Tash blinked hard. "You're… not going to kill me?"

"Waste of effort," Anukat said. "Not going to bring Pitt or Gert back. I'll hear you're dead in a gutter soon enough, I expect."

"I saved this whole fucking city! Show some bloody gratitude!"

"You're a lying little shit-stain," Anukat said. The big axe-man adjusted his filthy armour, slung his axe casually over his shoulder, winced, limped off.

"What are you going to do?" Lashiahar called after him. Don't go, she wanted to shout, don't walk off. You can't leave me with all these dead bodies and ruins and guilt.

He shrugged, didn't bother to turn to look back at her. "Enlist in the Tsarii army, obviously. Where do you think Feylash ran off to first chance she got? You guys are hardcore. Who doesn't want to be on the side that can raise the bloody dead? If Tash killed the king and all... I'm a bloody Tsarii hero, right?" He gave them both a cheerful wave as he jogged round the corner. "See you around, Tsarii, human skid-mark. Enjoy your triumph."

"I have... a demon... under my command..." Tash said, very, very quietly, once Anukat was out of earshot. "A demon, Anukat."

"Had," said Lashiahar. She walked over to where Tash was sitting. Bent down, yanked his hair so he was staring up at her. Kissed him hard on those pretty-boy pouty lips. "You are the worst assassin I've ever had the misfortune to meet. And I'm old enough to be your mum. If there was an intact wall within forty feet of here, I'd have you up against it with your trousers round your ankles telling you to stick it in harder and faster than you've ever done before, then stick you hard right back. But there isn't so... go find something better to do with your life than failing to kill people." She stroked his pretty cheek. Always had a thing about pasty skin. "'Human skid-mark'. That's good."

She heard him cough as she walked away in the opposite direction to Anukat. Like Anukat, she didn't look back. For a horrible moment, she thought he might follow.

After a horrible moment, she realised he wasn't going to.

* * *

SHE'D GOT ABOUT twenty paces away from the whole bloody catastrophe when she turned a corner and stopped short, heart pounding with shock as the realisation hit. Three year's work, night and day, training, planning, researching, dedicating her whole damned life day in day out to it. Really, some balloons or a banner or something would have been nice. And now it was done. Over. Like Thaliates Day presents and turkey: all that work, all that anticipation, and that's it, over and done, leaving you deflated. You can't get the first-time childhood magic back. I suppose, Lashiahar thought, I suppose I should find my unit now. Report in. One demon successfully distracted—maybe not quite the way we planned, but ultimately very successfully: check. What do you want me to do next then, boss?

The Tsarii restaurant was up and running, tasty home-from-home smell of well-spiced roast cat. Three Tsarii soldiers congratulated the chief on his cooking while supervising a group of Sharaami prisoners-of-war shovel a huge pile of re-dead dead bodies into a pit. Tsarii soldiers, Sharaami soldiers, Tsarii camp followers, Sharaami civilians, dogs, cats, rats, pigeons, a few very determined fish.

"Look at this helmet. Ancient history, this is. Must have been dead for, like, a thousand years or something. Think I'll take it home with me."

"You what?"

"Put it on the table by the front door. Keep stuff on it." Pause. "Once I've rebuilt the table and the front door and the house, obviously."

"I can't believe I survived all that shit. Keep pinching myself to check I'm not dead. You believe that crap about the giant undead octopus?"

"Mate: what do you think?"

"And the dumpy little woman killing machine?"

"I'm more likely to believe in the friggin' octopus. Some people'll say anything."

A lot of things she might have done differently. A lot of things she might feel shame or guilt or remorse about. But she thought: the walls are broken. People can get out of this shithole. That's got to be worth something, right?

Gods, her knees were aching something chronic. But… it's possible, she thought, that the ache and the limp might less to do with impending old age than with the fortune in gold pieces hidden inside her boots. The sky was clearing, she looked up and for the first time in, what, months? she could see the real bright yellow not-sickly-green-cancer-terrifying warm on her face spring sun. From an open window, a woman's voice warbled out that 'Obsidian Hearts' song. *She's got a black stone heart, and she dreams in blood... She's like a woman with a sword when all the knives are broken.* Lashiahar found she was humming along. Still thought it sounded better in the original Tsarii. The singer seemed positively cheerful, like things were actually looking up for her. And, yeah, when was the last time you could open a window in Sharaam without fear of alchemical gas clouds wafting in? Maybe Lashiahar regretted that kiss with Tash, what with the taste of vomit it had left in her mouth, but even that... Listen to those guys there in the work-gang. Sounded positively chipper about things. *One big happy nation under one monarchy, Tsarii and Sharaami united to build a new future, stronger together than we could ever have been apart! No more wars between us, no more fears of invasion, swords into ploughshares and that... Sharaam was always part of Tsarr, always would be. Everyone in Sharaam can have a nice peaceful life, richer, better, happier than before, if they simply remember that truth.*

I mean... Pitt and those guys: they were so damned rude about this city, it's not like they can have cared about it much? As for what they said about their king... They were happy to set up his assassination, for Thaliates's sake. What can Tsarii rule matter to them?

Spend a bit of the gold here, she thought then. Buy some stuff, get a few shopkeepers back on their feet. The city's population had... halved, maybe, in the last few hours? So rather fewer people around to buy stuff. Splash some cash around to some desperate widows and orphans, "*Look, not only are you at peace now with a strong law-enforcement presence on the streets to look after you, but you can sell me stuff for good Tsarii gold. How grateful are you?"* Or just get the hell out of here herself, go and find somewhere exotic where the sun shone and the dead were guaranteed to stay dead.

Nah. I'm a soldier, and my army just won. Years, I worked for this. Years! Go find my unit now. Report in. They'll be pleased with my performance. Promotion. Pay rise. I can give them… half the gold back, even. She could imagine her boss's face as she explained everything. *"I successfully distracted the demon. I, uh, proactively line-managed the man who stopped the out-of-control spell [I assume you're all feeling a bit guilty about using it; learning point there, guys, I hope—don't say that bit]. And I did it all at a cost that was substantially below budget."* Impressive! She'd been doing this lone secret agent role for a while now: maybe she could push for her own team, a leadership role. Hadn't Anukat had said he was planning on enlisting? She briefly imagined herself overseeing a new legion of Sharaami troopers, training them up in proper Tsarri military discipline. The itch she'd felt all this time, watching them flail around being led that badly. Almost wanted to march right up to the walls sometimes, take command, tell the wretched saps up there what they should be doing to defend their city.

The big secret, that you boys seem to be failing to grasp here, the big secret is that you need to kill them before *they can kill you. Waiting till it's the other way round… that's not really much use.*

Headquarters would be setting up in the empty space the palace had occupied before whatever happened to vaporise it happened. Lashiahar started walking fast in that direction. The last few days had been a shit-rag, yeah. But the more she thought about it, the happier she felt. Positive spring in her step now that everything was over.

Should have had Tash up against the wall, though, she thought. You almost never got that combination of dirty-blond haired and pasty skin in Tsarr.

She took five steps, turned a corner… and came face to face with the Shroud. Its tattered wrappings looked more like an, uh, shroud, than ever. Tattered skin-itch yellow of something old and rotted.

"Lies," the Shroud said. Even her beautiful voice seemed worn out, dried out. "Rot. Death. Peace."

Oh please. Not this again. I'm too bloody tired for this. I won; you lost. Magic yourself off. Lashiahar pointed in the direction Anukat had taken. "What's left of your crew went that way. Unless you're looking for Tash, if you've got the energy left to be bothered to kill him: in which case you'll find him hiding in an alley over there, covered in seagull shit." The problem, Lashiahar thought suddenly, was that *I employed a crew with this thing in it. Pitt listening to this thing rambling on should have been a big red flag when I first considered hiring him.*

"I'm sorry about Pitt," Lashiahar said.

"Tired," the Shroud said. "Guilty. Reluctant." She took a step forward. Her rags fluttered, Lashiahar braced herself for a decay-stink. This thing must be another undead or something. But... Lashiahar tried to peer through the wrappings. She had seen... she could remember... A woman's face, strong and healthy—surely she'd seen that, very briefly, beneath the Shroud's drapes, when the Shroud had done whatever she did. As the Shroud moved, she heard a sound, like a human footstep. A human quality in the way she moved her body, her cowled head.

"Pity," the Shroud said. "Gertri the Shield. Pitt the Sword. Strong and good. Kind to me." Look closer: Lashiahar was sure now she could see grey eyes hidden in the tattered wrappings. The curve of a woman's forehead. "A shield," the Shroud said. She seemed to sigh. "She killed Gertri. But she begged me to help her. She was so..." The Shroud seemed to pause, thinking. "She was so sad," the Shroud said at last. "Wanted. So much. Free. Happy. She wanted... peaceful," the Shroud said.

"She?" Lashiahar's mind spun. "What did you...? You banished the demon?"

The Shroud laughed in a peal of music so beautiful and joyful that Lashiahar wanted to laugh herself. "All this dying," the Shroud said. "The Third Worst Assassin saved the world. You hired him. I did nothing. Told her the truth. Let her go. She begged and begged to be let go."

"You banished the demon."

The Shroud was talking more clearly. Properly. Like an actual intelligible human person. Her body seemed so much more solid, a woman's strong muscled legs and torso beneath the tattered wraps. What had Anukat said? She's half here, half in the past, and half in the future.

"What are you?" Lashiahar said. "What did you do?"

Grey eyes very much like Lashiahar's own regarded her sadly. Strong large hands spread in a kind gesture beneath the corpse-yellow cloth. "She was a prisoner. I set her free," the Shroud said. Her voice less beautiful, rough and tired, but kind. "That's all."

"But—"

The... the *woman* shook her head. Laughed again. A very common normal sort of a laugh. "But nothing. That's all."

Just... two people standing in a street together.

Lashiahar said slowly, "Look, uh, Wint, we don't have, uh, Shrouds in Tsarr... I mean... if you..."

Wint was silent.

"It's... I mean... he'd pay..." Lashiahar stared at the ground. "I mean, what with... you know... you having lost... Be a really good opportunity for you..."

A sound behind them made them both start. Lashiahar found that she had her sword out. Undead giant octopus monster soldiers Tash sweet Thaliates kill them!

"No need," the Shroud—Wint—said. "Don't be afraid."

"I'm not afraid," Lashiahar spat back.

Two children regarded them with huge eyes. A girl, well-dressed, soot-stained, her chin raised with distain; a younger boy, bruises on his cheeks, beggar-thin.

Lashiahar tried to force herself to lower her sword. Couldn't. These children, sweet Thaliates, they weren't frightening, no. They were absolutely bloody terrifying.

"We were leaving," the girl said. "Now the walls are broken, we can leave. We walked nearly to the walls before, but there were all those nasty dead things. Poor things. But then we saw you, and we thought, Mye and me, we thought maybe you'd like to come with us?" Her eyes were green-red, like green glass in firelight, a broken bottle thrown into a bonfire. "Mye knows a good place where we could live, if you'd like."

The little boy nodded solemnly. "I went there once for a visit with my old mummy," he said. "It was very pretty. It had lots of trees."

"I—" All the gods, Lashiahar's mind screamed at her, run. Run. Run. *These two are worse than the dead.* The girl looked quizzically at her, cold, questioning, and inside the child's gaze Lashiahar saw another faceless, eyeless, open wound face. All the pain and fear and hurting: *my mother's dead, my father's dead, my brother's dead. Homeless. Helpless. All my life destroyed.* So young, a child merely—think, Lashiahar, what you were at her age, how bold, how innocent. And the things this child must have seen…

"I—" *Tash,* Lashiahar wanted to scream. *Anukat. Tash. Someone. Anyone. Help me.*

But: "I'm not talking to you, stupid," the little boy said.

"Stupid," the girl said.

Wint stepped forward to meet the children. "That sounds very pretty," Wint said. "I would like to come with you very much." She put her arms on the children's shoulders, exactly like any mother holding her children to keep them close.

"My old mummy and daddy talked a lot about how nice it would be for me to leave Sharaam," the boy, Mye, said. "Nice fresh air and clean water, they said. We were going to leave, but then the Tsarii came and we couldn't, then my old mummy and daddy died."

"I'm sorry your mummy and daddy died," Wint said. She seemed to look both at the boy and at Lashiahar. "I'm so sorry, Mye."

"Yes." The boy squeezed his eyes shut.

"Did you see the magic lady?" the girl said. "She was very sad, wasn't she, mummy?"

"She was, yes," Wint said. The children nodded gravely. "She's gone away somewhere better now," Wint said. "Like we will."

Mye tugged at Wint's hand. "Come on, then! I want to see the trees!"

Briefly, Wint looked at Lashiahar. Kind eyes with bags under them, wrinkles around them, in a kind tired plain face. "Weakness only," Wint said. "Remember, Lashiahar?"

"I don't understand."

"No," Wint said. "You wouldn't."

The three of them walked off slowly in the direction of the walls, the children chattering excitedly about sticks and conkers and beetles, Wint making sounds of interested agreement. Wint had long hair down her back, yellow-greyish; thick legs; she was dressed in trousers and a shirt and boots like any person. Her wrappings moved in the air, hung around her and the children, became a cosy-looking blanket.

The girl said, "Things will be better now, won't they, Mummy?"

Lashiahar strained to hear Wint reply, "Yes, they will be." She was sure from the way the girl skipped beside Wint that Wint had said yes. But Lashiahar was too far away to hear it.

She shivered.

Weakness only…? Well, yeah, you're a fucking Shroud *and you're walking off to be a mum to two stupid whiny kids.*

She tried to think again: *They should all be bloody grateful. Your city's no longer under siege, you've got peace and freedom, everything will be better now you're ruled by Tsarr. Who won here, hey? I did. Me.*

All three of them had drawn back away from her, Lashiahar realised. Looked at her, kept away from her, like she was the frightening one.

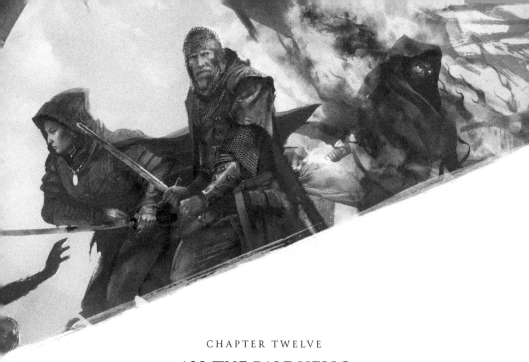

CHAPTER TWELVE

ALL THE PALE HELLS

S HE IS STANDING in a garden. Pink blossoms crown her, the
ground beneath her feet rises and falls as it breathes and speaks.
Faces rise from the surface, press up with mouths open. She
is standing in a clearing in a forest, ten human paces perhaps from
edge to edge. Iananr's feet sink into the damp earth, beads of dew
sweet on her skin. The trees reach out their branches to her, black
fingers, the trees rustle, whisper to her as if they are laughing.

In the west, the woodland runs steeply uphill, above
the tree line the hillside is thick grass rising to a
great crag of white bone-rock, vivid and vast
against the silver sky. To the east and
the south, the land spreads in a

wide wooded plain. To the north, she knows, in a little while she would come to a river, slow and meandering in sinuous coils, its banks like long curls of hair as it nudges its way between the trees. The woods beyond the river will end in yellow fields, beyond that will be a city where the houses are made of clear, sharp glass. The river will make a great loop, called back by the city's music, flow slow and sluggish close to the city's main gate. A day's journey beyond the city, the river will spill itself into marshlands that reek of salt, flesh there too thick to move through, the water will grow clotted. The marshes will turn at last into boiling grey sea.

The suns are high in the sky to the west behind the bone-crags. Iananr raises her face to them, feels their warmth. Real warmth. Real light. She turns quickly and her shadow stretches out behind her, writhes on the earth baring long teeth. Grass sharp as knife blades withers beneath her shadow's mouthing, grows up again thick, lush, rich.

She begins to climb the hill. It takes her a long time, running sometimes for the sheer pleasure of it where the hill is steep, stopping to admire the way the light falls through the leaves of a particular tree. In one place, white rocks come up to the surface still half-alive, opening and closing with a crunch of teeth. A stream runs down here, a little trickle of red where rain has fallen or where the flesh here still bleeds. She bathes her hands in it, wondering at the way it feels. When she reaches the top the air has a different taste to it, out of the smell of the trees. She sits with her back to a sheer face of bone. The ground is dry here, grey soil that crumbles when she rubs it between her fingers. Against her back, the bone is warm, she can feel it pulse. She stretches herself out, huge, flowing into the earth and the bone-rock, reaching up into the summer sky. Her body unfolds; her shadow unfolds itself.

Tiny figures move high in the sky, outlined white against the suns. Lovers, family, friends. Iananr thinks: soon I will go to join them, fly with them. From up here she can see the glass city as a winking shift of light as the glass breaks, reforms, breaks. She has a palace there, its floors jagged, its chambers a drift of perfume and birdsong. A garden with a fountain and many trees in flower, all made of mageglass in which she can watch and watch her body's reflections. A ballroom with a floor of diamonds on which she can sink into the pleasure of the dance. A many-columned temple, marble and silvery pearls, dedicated to herself.

A dry stalk of grass is itching her where it pushes its way up against the bone-rock. It stabs awkwardly into her back. She shifts position, finds a more comfortable place. One of the figures in the sky breaks away from its fellows, spirals towards her. She does not move but waits, eager, contented, to greet her lover, her kin, her friend.

As the goddess flies close she can hear the beat of its wings, feel the wind of its coming. A voice calls out to her, eager: "Rianan! You have returned to us! Rianan, my sister, my friend!" Long tendrilled arms embrace. Waves of pleasure wash over her. Golden, soft. Her body rends itself open. Pain blossoms. Fingers and mouths feed.

"Oh we have missed you, Rianan, my love."

Afterwards, she stretches herself out on the bloody grass beneath soft shadows, to sleep in peace.

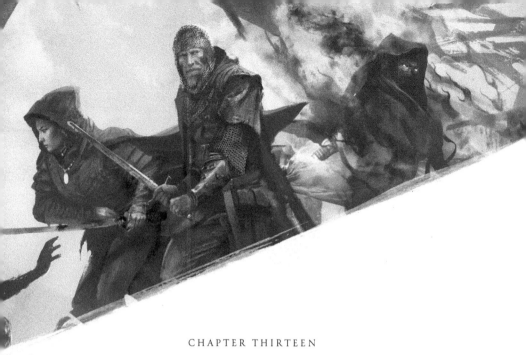

CHAPTER THIRTEEN

IN THE SHADOW OF THEIR DYING

TASH WATCHED LASHIAHAR leave with what might best be described as mixed emotions. The kiss was nice but who the hells did she think she was to reject him? Didn't she know she was *old*?

He frowned, brow crinkling as he struggled to decide what he felt. Go find something better to do with your life than failing to kill people?

I saved the city! I had a demon begging at my feet on a leash! I said 'kill' and she killed it! I saved—

What the hells had he done?

"You failed to kill the king!" he shouted after Lashiahar, but she was long gone. Long, long gone.

It would have been a great quick-witted comeback had it been quicker. And perhaps a tad wittier, he admitted.

Anyway, it was easy for her to say hurtful shit like that. She was a spy. She had a job. A career, even.

What have I got in my life? A few years before I inherit my dad's bald spot.

That was depressing.

What do I do now?

Even the rather sad title of Third Best Assassin was likely out of reach. Not that there was anyone left in Sharaam worth killing.

I'm useless. Yeah. Tell me something I don't know. You think anyone wants a life as a failed contract killer?

He used to help his dad lay bricks before he realized killing and stealing were both easier and more lucrative. The city was in ruins. Plenty of work for a brick layer.

Spend my life carting bricks. Put down the rent on some new lodgings. Would the entire city being in ruins lower rent or increase it? *Find Simonsi, go down on my knees and tell her how sorry I am, beg her to forgive me, ask her if we can start again.*

His right hand was hurting: he looked down and noticed a slither of glass still embedded in his thumb from where he'd broken the necrot spell and saved the whole city IS ANYONE LISTENING I SAID FROM WHEN HE'D BROKEN THE NECROT SPELL AND SAVED THE WHOLE CITY. He flexed his hand the way you might, say, hold a beer mug/an assassin's blade/a brick layer's trowel. The wound on his thumb looked like an erect cock.

Great. Just great.

Tash turned in a circle, trying to get his bearings. Everything looked different when it was on fire or heaped in a chaotic pile of rubble. Or both. Recognizing Tsepsis Street, he set off toward The Dripping Bucket. After a few steps, he stopped.

It's gone.

Was it weird that the destruction of the Bucket saddened him more than his own failures?

The thought of not drowning his sorrows in ale and a willing woman was too depressing.

Flet, An, Acol, all of them, they were all...

Gone.

Turning, he set off toward the docks. Scene of his greatest triumph. Revisit it. Gloat. *I'm the third best assassin in Sharaam. I saved this city, you know. Someone somewhere should be grateful. Yes?*

He took a few steps.

Yes?

Nope.

Another few steps, and he stopped again, an idea clawing at the back of his skull.

"The Rianican Church."

Beer. That whore who offered to give him a bath.

But that wasn't it.

He said out loud, "Collins said the Shroud didn't like the place because of all the dead gods begging her to let them out of the third basement."

He also said he built a wall over the entrance. Collins, who poured beer and who had never been a brick layer.

All the dead gods?

The demon served me because she thought I killed her previous master.

She wasn't quite grateful, but he couldn't find another word.

So, if I free the gods from their prison, won't they also be grateful?

Tash considered his options. Really, when you stepped back and examined them with an open mind—return to working for his dad or wake a few dead gods—it wasn't like he had a choice.

Collins is a lazy cunt.

At best, he piled a few bricks and slathered them with substandard mortar. Probably already crumbling.

Maybe Tash no longer had a frumpy demon serving him, but being served by grateful dead gods would probably be better!

Tash once again set off, heading toward the Church. He'd find a sledgehammer or a shovel or a pry bar on the way.

"Underestimating me," he told the world, "is a mistake."

* * *

HE JOGGED OVER to the Church in his excitement. More than excitement: rage and pride running through him. He thought he saw Anukat, briefly, tramping through the streets looking almost purposeful. *That blood in Anukat's beard, it occurred to Tash with revelatory force, I bet it's fake. He just wipes raw meat on his beard every morning for effect.*

When he reached the Church, Tash almost ran inside, then stopped and took several deep breaths, tried to comb his hair down. Right. On three. He slid nonchalantly through the doorway into the bar. Breathed in that warm beery scent. The Church didn't look in too bad a shape, all things considered. Three Tsarii soldiers hunkered down in the corner, one of them drinking from Anukat's bucket, Collins humming while he mopped a table down. *"Black stone hearts... broken knives... the more it snows, tiddly pom..."* The old man broke off when he saw Tash. "It's you? You're... still alive?"

"Thanks for the vote of confidence." *Still alive, still the third best assassin in Sharaam, still got great cheekbones.* His thumb spasmed with pain. *And a scar shaped like a willy, thanks for the reminder.*

Collins grinned. "I hear they're handing out medals to everyone who survived this morning with all major body parts and/or sanity intact."

"Yeah, well..." Collins hadn't got a scratch on him. Neither had the Tsarii soldiers. Gods, somehow that was the last straw. *That cunt Col-*

lins! I saved this city, and you're astonished I'm even alive! Any last doubts Tash had been harbouring vanished. *Dead gods, here we come! And then they'll see. Feylash, Lashi- Lasj- that spy bitch, Collins, Anukat—they'll all see! I'll show them power! I'll show them fear! I saved this city, and now this city will tremble before me!* Tash fiddled with the crowbar hidden beneath his jacket. His thumb was really hurting now. Collins headed upstairs to check on his girls. Quick as an eel, hair flicking elegantly over his shoulder, Tash slipped behind the bar. "Just going for a slash," he muttered to the Tsarii, who merely shrugged.

Behind the bar was a set of stairs down into the beer cellar. In the back of the cellar was a badly mortared brick wall.

He could almost hear them snoring.

Raised the crowbar.

Thin brick wall, badly mortared, and the air on the other side of the wall was thick and stank. Tash peered in the dark and he could see... something. The air swirled. As if something behind the wall was... forming.

Some things.

Eyes in the dark. Shape-shadows. A warm sense of sleep. Like a nest of kittens. Gods, it felt peaceful. For a moment, Tash though he should leave them to it. Or join them in sleeping. Curl up there behind the wall with them.

They felt so happy, sleeping. Snuggle up with them.

No.

Simonsi would be begging him to take her back. Feylash would be begging to share him with Simonsi, and Lashi- Lasi- the Tsarii spy would be begging to share that share with Feylash. Anukat would bow to him. Everyone in Sharaam would bow.

I SAVED THIS WHOLE POXY CITY!

I HAD A DEMON ON A FRIGGING LEASH!

YOU WILL ALL BOW TO ME!

Also he'd never be able to sleep with the pain in his stupid thumb. It hurt so much now the skin around the shard of glass seemed to be turning green.

So... Deep breath. He thought: How do you wake up a god?

Inspiration seized him. He shouted, "I'm here to rescue you!"

The basement echoed. *Ou ou ou ou ou.* The air was thick as oil and tasted wet. Lights flickered, star-like, a thousand years away and in Tash's face. Shadows—moving. Growing.

Unfolding.

Eyes blinked. Arms stretched. All the dead gods, fresh woken from sleep. They looked dreamily up at Tash.

He shouted in panic, "Come on, then! Wake up! Get up! Be—" *grateful.*

The dead gods yawned.

Rushed out of the third basement without a second glance at Tash.

He was still standing there, feeling... whatever the word might be when a god totally ignores you (like a normal human being, perhaps?) when the Church fell on top of him.

A Knife, an Axe, a Sword, a Shield, an undead kraken, a demon off her leash. But the worst of all this world's many perils, it turned out, was a load of badly mortared bricks.

In the shadow of so much dying ...

there's always something worse.

ACKNOWLEDGEMENTS

Thanks first off to Adrian and Fletch for helping me write something this insane. Iananr is a glimpse into the depths of my soul, and it feels kind of nice to get her out into the world for all to see. Like Marith and Thalia, she's lived in my head in different forms for years, it's nice others can meet her too now.

Thanks as always to Quint Von Canon and Stas Borodin, whose art has inspired so much of my writing. Sometimes it seems like they can see through my eyes as I'm writing, in fact, they capture what I see so well. (That should be terrifying, thinking about it.)

All the usual suspects, the writers, reviewers, bookvbloggers and fan sites that have supported me over the years. John Mauro and daughter at Before We Go Blog deserve a special mention for their support this year, as does the Beard of Darkness. Thank you all!

And finally—the people who bid in the BFS for Save the Children auction. The grimdark community excelled itself in its enthusiasm and generosity, as I knew we would. Grimdark for the bright and noble! You're heroes, people!

—ANNA SMITH SPARK